Alien Atira

Arlene Adamo

First Printing, 2020

ISBN 978-0-9810562-4-1

www.arleneadamo.com

To my wonderful loving husband
who has always supported my need to write

You can whisper love into a man's ear, but it doesn't mean he knows what to do with it.

That is the tragic part. The part that wears me out. The part that leaves me feeling as though it's all so useless. All this work, all this trying, and so little to show for it. My Naomh, why have you sent me here? What good can I do when there is no one who will hear me? No one to understand. All this love and nowhere to put it. No place to let this love thrive. It's killing me, holding it all in. It's killing me! Have mercy, Naomh! Have mercy!

This blue sky above me seems to hold promise, but this land… this land is so rife with the power of Moloch. I have travelled such a long way and have looked everywhere on this planet. Once I thought I found something…someone. But that was a fantasy. Not real. No one. No place to put all this love. It hurts having to hold it all in. It hurts.

Is it time yet? Can I leave this world? Can I return to you? Is it time to give up and let you destroy it? This is an unkind planet and I have grown so weary of its cruelty. I am having difficulty mustering up hope in the way I used to. Maybe the weight has become too much. You sent me here and yet I have found nothing I can do…no way to help. The injustice! The violence! All the filth of Moloch that coats this place! How can I look at any of it anymore? How can I stand to look at it knowing there is nothing I can do? Without some way to release upon the land this love I hold, how can Moloch be defeated?

In desperation, I have clung to things I should not have. I clung to *him*. For that, I ask forgiveness. But I have been true. I have hidden my true self away as you instructed and have borne the weight of it. At times, as you instructed, I showed them small glimpses of who I am, but it didn't matter. None of them could see. None of them knew me. They could not see. It's what they wanted. That was easiest for them…easiest for *him* too. Are these aliens so dull and horrible that they would mindlessly cling to Moloch who imprisons and tortures them? There is nothing here for me to save! Take me home! Please send the ship to take me home now!

CHAPTER 2

*L*ittle Rairai ran wildly down the sandy beach chasing after the wolar. The wolar was a hazy and obscure creature he had once conjured up from a daydream. No one could see her except for him. This made her special and made Rairai special too. An invisible world with an invisible friend that only he could visit. "Come back here!" he shouted as he zigged and zagged comically along the shore. He could see she was fast and cunning, taking many an unexpected turn. At one point, he was almost ready to give up trying to catch her when suddenly she paused to stare at a glittery rock. Wolars are known to be intrigued by all things that glitter. "Aha, you shall be mine," he whispered quietly as not to frighten her away. It was then that he pounced! Wrapping his arms tightly around her warm soft body, he exclaimed, "I have you now, and I will hold you forever!"

It surprised him when he felt her start to fight back. Not wanting to let her go, he held on tight, losing his balance and falling. For several moments, they wrestled in the sand. At one point, she scratched deep into his leg and his eyes began to tear up. "Look what you did to me!" he cried, and the wolar stopped squirming and kicking. She looked at his leg, and then began to weep herself. Wolars are like that…highly empathic.

Rairai saw her tears and felt bad about trying to capture her. Maybe he deserved it, having treated her like he did…pouncing on her…trying to subdue her. "Forgive me for holding you down," he apologized. "I am only a foolish boy who does foolish things."

At that point, she looked into his eyes and could see that he was being sincere. Her own fiery eyes changed from red to green and she pressed her warm snout gently against his cheek.

Rairai then carefully wrapped his arms around her once again. She did not fight with him this time. "You must not hurt me," he said. "I love you, wolar. You are mine and I am yours. We will be friends and that way we never have to be alone." He then happily carried his invisible companion back to where his family were resting around their picnic fire.

"Just lie to him Rairai," Twydi told him. "He won't know the difference and we'll get our money. It's what you do best, so do it!"

Rairai wasn't sure. This was no ordinary sucker. This was one of the Noblatjs and Rairai had been taught to respect them as authority. As early as he could remember, he was told their blood was clean… pure. They were the ones who ruled over the Lessers. The Lessers blood was tainted, making them unsuitable for anything other than the ordinary. Rairai was a Lesser. How could anyone ordinary cheat a Noblatj and get away with it?

"We're in too deep now," said Twydi. "You either follow through with this or we will be caught and both of us will be put to death. There's no backing out."

"But he's a Noblatj. He will know. His blood will tell him. You should have told me at the beginning who we were dealing with. Now look where we are. No place to go. How can we fool him? His blood is pure. His blood will tell him!"

Twydi moved a little closer, looked him straight in the eye and said, "Pull yourself together and think Rairai. We don't know what his blood will tell him. So far, it's told him nothing. Like I said before, I think this whole blood thing is just a story anyway. The fact is, he knows nothing, and what's more, there's no going back. You have to admit there's no going back. So, let's just finish this deal. You need to step up. You're the only one who can do it. Not me. I'm good only for the rough stuff. I'm not smooth and I don't have the art of persuasion the way you do. Everything depends on you now."

Rairai was angry that Twydi had gotten him into this situation. He was used to surprises from his business partner, but a Noblatj? This was way beyond anything they had ever dared attempt before. It was frightening. He wanted more than anything to back out, but he knew Twydi was right. There was no going back. You can't simply walk away from a Noblatj and not be ruined for life. His only hope of survival was to move forward. Twydi had entangled them both and now he had to face it head on. "Okay," he relented, "I'll send a request for a meeting."

"When?"

"I'll contact his office today."

"Good," said Twydi. "But remember to go in there with confidence. Stop thinking about his blood. If his blood could tell him anything, it would have by now. That blood thing is a load of grazzy dung. You've got nothing to worry about."

Rairai tried to feel reassured, but it was not easy. Just the idea of trying to cheat a Noblatj left him feeling a little sick to his stomach. He didn't know how he was going to get through it, but he knew he had no choice now. Twydi had gotten them in deep this time. Take a deep breath, he thought to himself, just a deep breath and we can get through this…we have to.

CHAPTER 3

"I am a maniac for love," she said. "Does that make me a fool?"

"What?" snapped the check-point agent.

"I am a maniac for love," she said again. "Does that make me a fool? Have I failed because of it?"

"Uh…look, I don't need anymore crazy Lessers today. Just don't cause any trouble and show me your identification."

Atira opened her hand and the agent quickly swiped her palm with the scanner. He then checked his screen, eyeing the data suspiciously. He felt something was not right about this one, but her identification registered as clear.

"Is there a problem?" she asked.

"No," said the agent, annoyed that there was nothing to substantiate his unsettled feelings. "Go through," he grunted, then motioned to the next person in line.

Atira walked through the turnstile and out into a large noisy waiting area full of people. I am alone, she thought as she looked around at all those who were being met by friends and loved ones. For a moment, the sadness almost overwhelmed her, but then she quickly choked it back. Alone is not bad. It is only different. I must leave all thoughts of *him* behind. I am still strong alone…maybe even stronger. My Naomh sent me here and I must finish what I started. It is my mission. It is my duty. I must go on.

Up ahead she saw the large blinking exit sign. Out there she knew she would find what she should have been looking for since landing on this planet. Too much time had been wasted already. She came here for one reason and she needed to follow through with it. So, without a second thought, she headed straight for those doors.

CHAPTER 4

Rairai fidgeted uncomfortably on the hard plastic chair. He had been sitting in the reception area for more than two hours. Before he arrived, he knew it was likely he would be forced to sit and wait for a very long time. That was normal treatment for a Lesser, but he didn't realize how stressful it would be. As time wore on, he found himself becoming increasingly anxious and began to wonder if the Noblatj had found out the truth and was now only torturing him before the kill.

He shifted forward on the chair and stared down at the floor. There was a faint stain on the tile beside his left foot. Is that blood? Perhaps it is the blood of the last Lesser who tried to swindle a Noblatj. Suddenly, it seemed as if the temperature in the room had jumped several degrees. Rairai wiped the sweat from his brow and loosened the collar on his Lesser best-suit.

Wanting to clear his mind of fear, he closed his eyes and tried thinking of nothing. Quickly realizing that wasn't working, he then began counting to ten, visualizing each number as a colorful painting. This was a trick he taught himself as a boy and it usually helped. When he reached ten, he opened his eyes and found himself staring at the receptionist who was busy working at the open panel of her console. 'Puffy face', he thought, secretly amusing himself to further relieve his anxiety. She has the puffy face. They're all getting it. They think it makes them look young…beautiful. It just makes them look puffy faced, and years from now when it's out of style and their faces are stretched out, they will regret it.

But this distraction did not last long as he found himself, once again, staring back down at the floor and the mysterious stain. The anxiety began to rise in his throat.

Quickly shifting his gaze over to the blank wall on his left, he tried to focus on happy memories from his childhood. This was his newer trick for overcoming fear…a trick that almost always worked.

He thought back to his precious wolar. His secret friend who no one else could see. How much fun they had together! Running! Chasing! Jumping! Climbing! Whenever he'd throw a ball against the wall, he'd imagine it was she, throwing it back again. The wolar was as real as anything to him back then. Sometimes, he preferred her to actual friends as she was more imaginative and far more trust-worthy. The two of them even created a funny little song together that they'd sing while they played. In all these years, he'd never forgotten it.

If you see the giant
Eat his bread
If you see the giant
Shake his bed
If you see the giant
Hit his head
If you see the giant
Kill him dead

"A-HEM!"

Rairai looked over at the receptionist and, seeing the annoyed look on her puffy face, suddenly realized that, as he was singing the song in his head, he had been unconsciously keeping time with his foot against the chair leg. The noise was irritating her. He promptly stopped and gave her an apologetic smile.

Just then, the door across from him slid open and a woman dressed in a white gown stepped out. He noticed she had a puffy face too. "Mr. Rairai Swyer?" she asked, her voice sounding mechanical and robotic.

She's had voice enhancement surgery, he thought. That was another fashion trend.

"Yes, I'm Rairai Swyer," he answered as he stood up and offered her his hand.

She ignored his offer and turning away said, "Please follow me."

Rairai followed her through the door and they proceeded down the long hallway, their heels clicking rhythmically against the shiny black floor. Click, clack, click, clack. On either side of the hall were gurgling lime colored waterfalls with hundreds of shiny little orange fish falling over and over again. Fishy, fishy, fish, fish. Rairai felt like he had entered some kind of bizarre fantasy land. Normally, he would find it delightful, but, given the circumstances, it made him even more nervous. What could he expect in this type of place? What was expected of him? What were the rules in such a strange and possibly deadly world?

The pulsating glow coming from the bright overhead lights was beginning to give Rairai a headache, and he wondered if they were an intentional torture for Lessers who dared walk these halls or if it was a mere technical glitch. Could a Noblatj's corridor have defective lights? Wasn't everything about the Noblatjs supposed to be perfect?

When they came to a set of shiny doors, the woman reached out and pushed a silver button on the wall. As they waited, Rairai stared at the holographic image displayed on the doors. It was an over-sized head of an imposing long-horned ram with angry eyes. It seemed to be charging forward out of puffy clouds. Puffy face, puffy clouds, puffy fluffy scary ram.

As he stood staring at the image, the ram's head suddenly split in two as the doors slid open. "Mr. Swyer," said the woman, gesturing for him to enter.

When he stepped inside the room, the doors quickly closed behind him and he found himself alone, at least he thought he was alone. It was much darker here than in the bright hallway, so at first, he could not see much. As his eyes adjusted, he realized he was in a spacious, mostly empty room. The walls were dark, possibly a gray color and the floor was made of dimly lit tile-lights. The floor then suddenly brightened, and he was now able to see the room fully. The walls were actually a brilliant vermilion and the ceiling an electric blue. At the far end was a large desk and chair...the only furniture. The desk, fashioned out of some type of a translucent material Rairai had never seen before, sat in an alcove which was full of paintings, hangings and shelves displaying sculptures of all sorts. It was well known that the Noblatjs took great pride in their private art collections and loved to display these treasures in crowded clusters. The legs of the desk were a brilliant red color molded in the shape of a woman's legs. Behind it was a ridiculously pompous tall gold chair. Rairai knew that the Noblatj's enjoyed flamboyant styles, but he still couldn't help feeling taken aback by the outlandishness of the designs. He also felt a little guilty for these thoughts.

"Hello Mr. Swyer."

At first, Rairai did not know where the voice was coming from, but then a figure stepped out from somewhere behind the alcove. As he came further into the light, Rairai could see this was indeed the Noblatj. His bleached white skin and long blue hair told him as much. The man looked quite young, but it was rumored that the Noblatjs received special injections under their skin to keep it tight, so it was hard to know for sure.

"Lofty Bitterridge?" asked Rairai, addressing him by his Noblatj title.

"Who else, Mr. Swyer, or may I call you Rairai?" When the man spoke Rairai caught a glimpse of his glowing blue teeth. Having your teeth colored in neon shades was the newest trend among the Noblatjs.

"I would be greatly honored, Lofty Bitterridge" Rairai smiled back, surprised a Noblatj would be so personable. He expected something much more severe and authoritative. "It is indeed my greatest privilege that you would meet with me. I am so very deeply, deeply honored." Rairai immediately felt embarrassed that in his nervousness he had used the words 'honor' and 'great' twice. He was usually a much smoother talker when it came to business.

Bitterridge took a seat in the chair and gestured for Rairai to come forward. Rairai walked towards the desk, but then stopped.

This, he guessed, would be the respectful distance. Any closer could be considered an insult and the meeting would be over. For days, he had studied the protocol, but he was still very worried that his knowledge of how to behave might fall short. If he accidently stepped beyond his place, the results could be disastrous. He now silently waited in the dim light, head bowed, for the Noblatj to speak.

The silence dragged on for what seemed like a long time. At one point, Rairai wondered if the Noblatj had left the room and was tempted to look up. Should he look? No, he must not look. He must wait…wait until the Noblatj speaks. The silence could be a test. A test of his patience and fortitude.

Finally, Bitterridge said, "So Rairai. I am told you have something interesting for me. What is it?"

Rairai looked up and, without making direct eye contact, said, "Lofty Bitterridge, I pray that you will consider this unique product developed by our very talented team of extraordinary researchers. It is a product beyond compare that is guaranteed to bring you greater riches and further adoration among the Lessers." He then reached into his pocket and pulled out the small elegant hand-carved red coral box. The box alone had cost them everything they had left plus a little more, but Twydi had told him that presentation was everything and he was usually right about that sort of thing. "This, great Noblatj, is what we have aptly named Heaven Sent," he said as he offered it in his outstretched hand.

"Come closer," said Bitterridge, obviously intrigued.

Rairai moved closer to the desk. He nervously held out the box as though he were offering a morsel of food to a dangerous beast. As he stood there with outstretched hand, he momentarily glanced up at the Noblatj. It surprised Rairai that the skin that looked so porcelain smooth from farther away, did not look so flawless up-close. It seemed to have a bumpy almost melted plastic texture that could not be fully hidden by the all too obvious makeup. Rairai was not prepared for this. From early on, he had been taught that the Noblatjs were perfect in every way.

Bitterridge continued to stare with fascination at the box. "What is it?" he asked.

Rairai then pressed the side of the box with his thumb, causing the lid to spring open and POOF! a tiny explosion of sweet-smelling purple dust flew up into the air, accompanied by three harmonic notes. TING! TANG! TONG!

The Noblatj jumped in surprise and Rairai immediately worried that startling him had been the wrong thing to do. But instead of being angry or annoyed he only giggled and then leaned in again for a closer look.

The dust had now dissipated and Lofty Bitterridge stared in wonder at the metallic red pill resting on the glowing purple lining. "This," Rairai explained, "is Heaven Sent. It is a wondrous unique pharmaceutical of extraordinary potential. Although some have dreamed of inventing such a thing, no one in history has ever been successful, that is, before now."

Bitterridge reached over and picked up the pill with his finger and thumb. He studied it closely then asked, "What does it do?"

"What does it do?" asked Rairai, so relieved to see that Bitterridge was interested. "What does it not do?" he added, relaxing into the sales pitch he had practiced endlessly in front of the mirror. "It rejuvenates! It resuscitates! It renews! It remedies! It reanimates. If something is too small, it enlarges! If something is too large, it reduces! What is too loose, it tightens! What is too tight, it loosens! When you need to feel grounded, it brings you down! When you need to feel higher, it takes you up! It is the quintessence, the embodiment of power, the great panacea, the elixir of elixirs! It is Heaven Sent!"

"Heaven Sent," Bitterridge whispered to himself as he continued to stare with wonderment at the pill he still held tightly in his fingers.

Rairai, finding himself feeling even more confident, added, "All of the scientific data substantiating the incredible medicinal value of this wonder drug can be sent to your offices today, if you are interested. There were many companies we considered as potential investors, but none even compared to yours, Lofty Bitterridge. You are, without a doubt, our very first choice and the best suited to deliver this miracle product to the Lessers."

"Yes, of course," the Noblatj agreed. "Your decision to come to me first was a wise one." He then looked Rairai in the eyes and gave him a big smile.

The sudden flash of those bright blue teeth was a shocking and unnerving sight. Rairai felt his skin crawl and his instincts told him to run. But he knew he couldn't. It was too late to turn back. So, he silently rebuked himself for being so silly and tried to focus only on the deal at hand.

CHAPTER 5

Atira walked along the row of expensive shops. Although she did not fit in with the fashionably dressed and surgically altered shoppers, they ignored her, assuming she was someone's maid on an errand. It was not as if a poor Lesser would ever dare to walk down these streets for any reason other than servitude. Such a thing would never be expected.

She stopped outside a small purple boutique with a sign that read **The Provider** in big glowing purple letters. In the window was a mid-length dress woven from thread made from the rare mahli plant...the finest thread available on the planet. As she looked closer, she could see the seemingly endless hues of deep reds, blues, purples, whites and greens, all interwoven with such delicate complexity that it was impossible for the naked eye to fully comprehend the artistry of the intricate pattern.

Atira then looked from the beautiful dress in the window and down at the drab beige dress she was wearing. It was not even hers. The clothes she had arrived in were lost. Somehow, she had misplaced them. So, when it came time to leave *him*, she had nothing to wear but the things he had bought for her. This was a problem because she didn't want anything from him. She wanted to make a clean break. So, she traded clothes with his maid. Now however, even the dress of his maid was proving to be too much of a burden. I must rid myself of all that he is. I must be free. For the sake of the mission, I must be free. It is necessary.

The moment Atira entered the shop, the saleswoman rushed up to her. "Oh goodness!" she exclaimed. "We must get you to the back room. You mustn't be seen here in the front. It could put off potential customers. Come with me." She then led Atira to the back of the shop and through a curtain to a dingy windowless stock room. "Now then," she said, "how may we be of service to your Mistress?"

Atira just silently stared at her.

The saleswoman began to grow impatient. "Are you unable to speak? Do you have a note from your Mistress? You must tell me what you want."

"The dress in the window," Atira replied.

"Oh, that dress! What a marvelous choice your Mistress has made. It is unique. The only one like it. Imported from the far shores of Frihet. It was woven by the great artisan, Dilagus Chir. It is a precious treasure indeed. Very expensive but worth it. Stay here and I will get it."

Atira waited and within a short time the saleswoman returned carrying the dress in her arms. She laid it out on a nearby table, removed her infolio from her pocket and tapped some information into it. She then asked, "Now tell me, what is the name of your Mistress?"

Atira walked over to the dress and ran her hand over the soft material. "Yes, this is very good," she said.

"What do you think you are doing? How dare you!" the horrified saleswoman shouted. "That is not your place! You never touch the things of your Mistress without explicit permission! Who trained you? I shall report this." She then reached out to grab Atira by the arm.

Atira stepped back before she could touch her. "You will not put your hands upon me," she said calmly. "I will not warn you again."

The saleswoman was in shock. Never had she come across any maid who would dare speak back like that. "I shall not only touch you, but I shall do your Mistress a great favour and beat you!" she exclaimed.

She raised her arm to strike, but before the woman's hand could come down, Atira drew her quantum-eraser from her pocket and, in a flash, the saleswoman instantly disintegrated. "I am no one's maid," Atira declared then turned back to the dress on the table. She ran her fingers over the fine soft fabric once more. There was no mistaking the perfection of the weave. It was certainly an anomaly on a planet of so much imperfection. Both beautiful and mathematically sound, there was only one possible place from which it could have originated. Her Naomh. Her Naomh had reached through from the other dimension and placed it here as a sign and as a gift. "Yes, this is what I need," she said as she picked up the garment and held it softly against her cheek. "Exactly what I need."

CHAPTER 6

A tira's new purple shoes made small tap-tap noises as she walked along the street. She had picked them up before leaving the shop, along with the saleswoman's infolio which was now securely tucked in her dress pocket. As she passed by the people on the street, it quickly became apparent that they saw her differently than they did before. No longer were they trying to avoid her, force her to one side or even glance at her with disdain. Now they were seeing a wealthy Lesser…one of them. This would be important for her to complete her mission.

I must eat, she thought as she came upon one of the more exclusive restaurants on the street. When she entered, the host hesitated to allow her in. He was trying to decide whether she was a worthy enough Lesser to eat in a place renowned for its Noblatjs clientele. Although the Noblatjs did not usually frequent the same places as even the wealthiest Lessers, there where certain establishments where they enjoyed the 'quaintness of roughing it'. It was considered fashionably risqué by some of them.

The host carefully looked her over. Her face did not look surgically altered and her hair was not done up in the latest style. This was suspicious. Was she truly the kind of Lesser that belonged in his restaurant?

As he stood there trying to assess her worth, Atira put her hand into her pocket and rested her fingers against the quantum-eraser. Eating was imperative.

After considering the current emptiness of the restaurant and the woman's extraordinarily expensive dress and shoes, the host finally decided it was safer to allow her in then to send her away. He had once before misjudged an eccentric wealthy Lesser and it almost cost him his job. He didn't want to make that mistake again. "Right this way, Mistress," he said with a bow.

He showed her to a small table in the corner. "No," Atira said. "I want that one." She pointed to the large table by the window.

"But Mistress, that is a table reserved only for the Noblatjs. You would be much more comfortable here."

"No," she said again. "That table is empty. I shall sit there."

Before he could stop her, she walked over and sat down.

The host wondered what he should do next. There were a group of Noblatjs at a table nearby, but they were busy eating and talking, and seemed unaware of what was going on. The host knew that if he were to make any sort of a scene, it could disturb their meal and possibly bring his establishment into disrepute. Noblatjs were very sensitive to anything that disturbed the quiet and order of things especially when they were eating. In the end, he decided it was less risky if he simply allowed the troublesome Lesser to sit at the table. The Noblatjs would likely not even notice her, and if they did, he'd come up with some sort of an excuse. He then handed Atira a menu with a forced but professional smile.

CHAPTER 7

Twydi waved the infolio in the air. "Did you see these numbers?" he cried. "Did you see them?"

"Yes," laughed Rairai. "I saw them."

"We did it! We are rich men! No more struggling! No more worrying! We made it! We beat the odds and officially became wealthy Lessers!" He slapped Rairai on the back. "What will you buy? I'm thinking of one of those big country properties. Lots of room. Lots of land. Maybe a grazzy or two. Can you see me? Out on my land. Riding my grazzy through the open fields like some hero in a Noblatj story."

Rairai plopped down in his favorite old worn out chair. "Before you go off riding on your imaginary grazzy, we must be certain that everything is in place. We don't want it to all go wrong."

Twydi laughed. "We've gone over it a million times. It's iron clad. Nothing can go wrong. We sell dreams my friend and we just sold a really big one. Everyone's happy. You make money. I make money. And Lofty Bitterridge is not only richer but can enjoy greater prestige among the Noblatjs. It's all perfect. Everybody wins!"

"And if they find out those scientific reports are bogus, then what?"

"Then my friend, Lofty Bitterridge is in so deep and is so much richer that he'll cover it up for us. He's not going to let this well run dry. The Noblatjs know how to work the system they set up. By having him sign with us, it insures against getting found out. Right now, all we need to worry about is how to spend the money, and I'm picturing a big house with a gold speckled grazzy in the yard. And maybe you should be thinking about buying a new chair."

"I hope you're right," said Rairai, "Not about the chair. I love this chair. But about it all working out."

"Would I lie to you, my friend?" grinned Twydi.

"You have before," replied Rairai.

"Only when necessary," Twydi chirped. "Only when necessary. But it's always worked out in the end, hasn't it?"

This was true. Rairai couldn't deny that Twydi's 'creativity' with the truth had gotten them places, but this was now so much bigger. They had everything to lose if it went wrong.

Rairai looked at his friend's big happy grinning face. It was so full of confidence…so sure of everything. *Listen to him. This is a good thing. Your dreams have finally come true. Try and enjoy it.* But no matter how hard he tried to convince himself that everything would be fine, Rairai just couldn't shake that unsettled feeling deep within.

CHAPTER 8

I t is here somewhere. I know it is...the house I secretly built from the other dimension. By building it through dimensional distance, I ensured that Moloch would not sense it and try to destroy it. I hid it in plain sight. Now, I know I am close. The coordinates are correct but where is it?

As Atira came around the bend in the road, she was surprised to find herself standing in front of an entrance to a walled wealthy Lessers' neighborhood. The large metal security gates were wide open, so she entered and proceeded down the tree-lined street past the row of stately manors and manicured gardens. She wondered what had happened. This wasn't what she was expecting. When she had built the house, there had been nothing here but trees. Since that time, others had built around it. Although this was not in the kind of place she was expecting, she knew it did not matter. Universal law had a way of working things out. There had to be a reason why it was this way. In time that reason would be revealed. Every mission is an unfolding fate.

As she passed by the houses, each one seemed dull and wrong. None of them were the one she was looking for. It was difficult to know exactly what the house would look like as appearances are different when looking through dimensions, but she had faith that it was here somewhere, and in her heart, she knew that, when she saw it, she'd recognize it.

Sure enough, as she reached the end of the street, there it was! Its peaked roof, tall windows and rounded balcony on the second floor looked so much different on this planet, but it was undoubtedly her house. Her instincts, although dulled by the weightiness of this Moloch infested world, were still able to tell for certain that she was in the right place.

As she approached the front door, she heard music coming from inside. This was not good. Someone had occupied her house. Someone with no right to do so. She tried to open the door, but it was locked. So instead, she rang the bell. Within moments a cheery maid answered. "Hello, how may I help you?" she chirped.

"I must see those who occupy this house," Atira replied.

The maid looked at her suspiciously, but then noticing the expensive dress and shoes thought better of it. "Please come in," she politely said as she moved aside.

Atira stepped over the threshold and looked around the spacious front foyer. Instantly, she felt her body relax in a way it had not done since arriving on this world. It felt good. After all she had been through, it felt so good to finally be in her own house.

"I will get my Master or Mistress. Please wait here," said the maid, then disappeared into another room.

Now alone, Atira stared up the white staircase in front of her. This was indeed her house, and up those stairs was a secret power...a hidden power from another world...her world. So, why had she not come here first instead of allowing herself to get distracted? How could she have let that happen? Now she just hoped she had not wasted too much time. There was so much to be done and so little time left.

As she began ascending the stairs, she heard a voice suddenly ask, "Where do you think you are going?"

She looked down and saw a man and then a woman staring up at her.

"Who are you and what business do you have in our house?" the woman demanded.

Atira did not reply. She simply stared down at the two. She could see that their clothing was very expensive. They had lived well in her house, but now she was here. They had to go.

"Call the police!" exclaimed the woman to the maid who stood nearby.

"Well, are you going to leave, or should we call the police?" asked the man, a little confused because her clothing was not that of a poor Lesser thief. He was beginning to wonder if she was perhaps suffering some sort of mental breakdown and had simply wandered away from her home.

Atira knew these people would not simply leave. They had no right here, but they had lived a good life in her house and would not give it up easily. She could see no other alternative. Her Naomh had specifically instructed her that if there is no other alternative, there is no other alternative, and she must do whatever is necessary to free the planet from Moloch. "The future of our universe depends upon it," he told her. So, reaching into her pocket, she took out her quantum-eraser and, before either of them could speak another word, they were disintegrated.

Atira then looked over at the horrified maid who was standing nearby. "I have no need for a maid," she said. "Do you wish to be free or do you prefer to meet the same fate?"

The maid, in shock and unable to fully process what just happened, stammered, "I...uh...free?"

"Then go," said Atira, "and tell no one."

The maid went quickly out the front door, closing it behind her.

Atira then looked back up the staircase. "Now, that I have gotten rid of the interlopers and have claimed my house, it is time to look upon the powerful heart I have placed at its center."

She continued to ascend the stairs, placing one foot after the other, each step feeling good...firm and solid. There were sixteen in all, each one carefully crafted according to very specific measurements. Everything in this house was created according to the same standard of perfection. That was crucial to her work. Even the smallest corner was mathematically sound so that the entire house might be fully synchronized with the positive energies of the universe.

When she reached the wide landing at the top, she then turned towards the front of the house and stood before the tall white double doors. Here she paused. Behind those doors was where her masterpiece was hidden. She could feel its powerful energy radiating from inside...penetrating her every atom...calling to her.

Atira did not want to open the doors right away. She wanted to savour this moment. Even though she had not been long on this planet, as some missions can take decades, it seemed as if it had taken forever to get to this point, and now finally, she was in the right place. The place where she could at last fulfill her mission. A precious moment of joy suddenly washed over her. It was a welcome taste of home.

After the moment had passed, she reached out and pressed the opening mechanism. The doors then gracefully slid apart. The first thing she noticed was that the occupiers had filled the room with garish faux-Noblatj bedroom furnishings...the style she knew was popular among wealthy Lessers. But even this could not dampen her mood. Instead, she ignored the outrageous ugliness of it all and tried to determine behind which wall she had hidden her masterpiece.

Realizing she would need the help of the sky to get her bearings, Atira walked over to the one-way transparency door at the far side of the room and slid it open. She then stepped out onto the balcony and looked up at the sky. It was not completely dark yet, but the two beautiful red moons were clearly visible. Noting their current coordinates, she was able to quickly calculate where in the room she needed to be looking.

Stepping back inside, she walked over to the wall opposite the bed and easily pulled away a heavy bright red cabinet and then pushed aside another large glassy blue one. She then removed all the decorations that were hanging on the wall. Once the area had been cleared, she opened her mind and envisioned the hidden panel. It was now clear to her where she had placed the mechanism. Pressing her palm against that secret spot, she watched as the as the wall instantly dissolved, revealing a control console unlike anything this world had ever seen. It was so sleek and simple that it looked as though it was nothing much at all, but Atira knew this was the most powerful machine on the planet. She walked over and slid her hand along its smooth edge.

Oh, how beautiful you are! This is what I should have come for in the beginning. This is what my Naomh instructed me to build and this…this is how I will defeat Moloch.

CHAPTER 9

Rairai checked the time on his infolio. Twydi was supposed to be meeting him here for a dinner meeting, but he hadn't turned up yet. It wasn't unusual for Twydi to be late, but this late? Of course, with all their new-found success, Twydi had become even less dependable than usual. In fact, he had become so busy searching for his dream home, as well as shopping for everything under the sun that he was neglecting the company. There were still so many things to work out, and with the business growing so fast, it was important to keep an eye on things. "The bigger you are, the easier it is for money to go missing. You just can't let things get out of control," he reminded Twydi many times, but to no avail. Twydi was Twydi and there was not much he could do about it.

Rairai took out his infolio from his jacket pocket and tapped in Twydi's private symbol. Immediately, it buzzed through, but there was no answer. The generic bot then appeared on the screen. Twydi had set it to 'alluring female' mode. *"Hello darling. Twydi is currently indisposed. Please leave a message and he'll get back to you as soon as he can. My darling, but you do have such sexy eyes."*

"Twydi, where are you? I've got more important things to do than to sit in this restaurant waiting for you. Get here now!"

"Is this the end of your message, darling?"

"Yes."

"Well, thank you. Twydi will get back to you just as soon as his very busy schedule allows. He is a very busy and a very sexy man."

Rairai signed off, ordered another drink and went back to reviewing the many pending contracts in his infolio. This was all he could do for now, being limited by what could be accomplished without his business partner. Before finalizing anything Twydi's official mark was needed. This was in their agreement with each other and with Lofty Bitterridge.

Having reviewed all of the contracts more than once already, it didn't take long for Rairai to finish. At this point, he decided he had enough of waiting and thought it best if he went looking for Twydi. There were several contracts that were supposed to be signed today and Lofty Bitterridge would be expecting the finalized copies. He had to get Twydi's mark on them. Tossing back what remained in his glass, he then transferred money from his infolio into the panel on the table to pay for the drink, adding a little extra for the inconvenience of him taking up the table for so long.

When Rairai stepped out into the street, he checked in both directions, hoping that maybe Twydi had decided to finally show, but there was no sign of him. He then decided the first place to look would be that over-priced apartment his friend had recently rented as a temporary place to stay while he searched for his dream home. It wasn't too far from the restaurant.

As Rairai headed in the direction of the apartment, he could feel himself getting more and more frustrated and angry. Twydi knows we have important work to do! How could he be so irresponsible! I swear if he's in there with a woman, I'm going to kill him!

CHAPTER 10

Atira stood on the balcony and stared up at the stars. She gave out a long deep sigh. *My Naomh is up there...at home...the comfort of home. I wish I were there too. This world is too empty. These aliens...too empty.*

The night wind had started blowing in colder and she thought about the storm that was on its way. It was going to be big. She knew that. "Force is sometimes needed for the renewal," she said, reassuring herself. She never liked this part. It made her feel almost physically ill, but she knew it was necessary. It had to be done. To fix what was broken, sometimes it had to be broken some more.

When deciding on how big of a storm it would be, she had taken into consideration every variable. *I have to hit them hard and in all the right places. They've left me with no choice. Renewal is imperative. They do not know how to renew on their own, and they will not listen to words. This is the only way.*

Slipping back inside the room, she walked over to the console. *The ones who had occupied...the ones she had to erase...they had no idea what was hidden behind that wall. It amazed her that, all this time, they could be living next to such an incredible and powerful machine, yet never even sense it. How dull are these aliens that they cannot feel such a beautiful thing as this? It embodies the* great design of my Naomh that connects to both this planet and the entire universe. I simply do not understand how they could be so unfeeling...so disconnected from something so wonderful. Moloch's presence breeds stupidity.

As her hand hovered over the console, she delicately did a little dance with her fingers, bringing up the holographic atmospheric oscillator. She then began to double check all of the settings. In her heart, she already knew they were correct, but in her head, she doubted. This was one of the negative effects of the Moloch tainted atmosphere, and then, of course, there was also what she had done with *him*. Those two things had caused a rift between knowing and instinct, leaving her forgetful and vulnerable to doubt and illusion. This was something she would have to fight and fight hard.

Her eyes quickly scanned the calculations. Yes, everything is in place. She then removed her hand and the screen disappeared. The countdown had now been activated.

Atira sighed. She knew many people would suffer from what was coming and sincerely wished there were a better way. If only they would listen to words, it wouldn't have to be like this. But words are not enough to make these aliens change. At this point, fury is the only thing they understand...fury and fear.

She then walked over to the large bed against the opposite wall and ran her hand down the elaborately carved bedpost. It was the only tastefully crafted piece in a sea of hideous furnishings. Atira looked closely at the beautiful artistry...its intricate swirling lines mixed with images of ancient mystical creatures. It was an amazing work of art, but at the same time it was also an unnecessary luxury and she knew it was important not to revel in luxuries. Indulgences were distractions that could interfere with her mission. Yet at that moment, she couldn't help feeling glad of it being there. She needed a comfortable place to rest...a beautiful place to rest...some place that could remind her of the wondrous feeling of home. Surely her Naomh would not begrudge her this one small thing when she was so in need of a little peace. After all she had been through on this planet, her mind and body needed this.

Kicking off her shoes, she then let her dress fall to the floor. As she stretched her arms wide, she felt free of the secrets that weighed upon her…of her disguise she was forced to wear. She felt more like herself again…light…unburdened…with no suffocating Moloch-filled gravity holding her down. Pulling back the smooth luxurious sheets, she climbed into the soft bed. How lovely it felt and how hungry she was to dream. Atira had not dreamt in a very long time… at least not the kind of dreams that could fill her. Tonight, she would feast. She would sleep through that terrible storm and feast upon beautiful dreams of love. Those dreams of love were all she really had to carry her through on this loveless planet. They alone were the promise of home on this cold alien world.

CHAPTER 11

Rairai tried the buzzer once again before pressing the door code. Twydi had given him the code *just in case*. "What if I'm being held captive by a swarm of adoring women and can't escape? I will need you to rescue me," he told him, and Rairai knew he was only partly joking.

"Twydi!" Rairai called before stepping in and sliding the door closed behind him. He walked down the short hall to the living area. "Twydi? Are you here?" There was still no answer.

Outside, the thunder boomed.

Rairai checked the bedroom next. The bed was a mess, but Twydi was never one to make his bed. He then checked the kitchen and found a freshly opened bottle of cya-drink and an empty glass, but nothing else.

He returned to the living area where he noticed Twydi's infolio sitting on a chair. Rairai picked it up. Where would he go without his infolio?

Suddenly, a loud bang made him jump, and he turned to see chunks of hail smashing against the windows and balcony door. A lightning storm at this time of year? Rairai had never seen hail that size before. The jagged white lumps were crushing Twydi's new sun lounger. Wherever his friend was, Rairai just hoped he wasn't caught in this bad weather.

Looking down at Twydi's infolio still in his hand, he wondered if he should open it. An infolio was considered a person's most private possession. Even those in committed relationships knew enough to respect one another's infolios. But this was possibly an emergency, and he would keep his snooping strictly to the messages and any appointment listed. Surely, Twydi wouldn't take offense given the circumstances. He'd forgive him.

Rairai knew he'd have no trouble opening the infolio. He'd seen Twydi tap in the pass code many times. It was *tnesnevaeh*...'Heaven Sent' backwards – ridiculously obvious, but that was Twydi. He could be very smart about some things, but not so smart about others.

The first thing Rairai saw when he opened the infolio was the standard weather warning that the Ministry of Meteorology had just issued.

Warning:
We are currently under a severe weather warning.
It is expected not to end until daybreak.
You are required to remain indoors until further notice.
Failure to do so will result in a fine and possible incarceration.
Safety first, citizens!

Rairai closed the page and went to Twydi's communication log. At the top of the list was a message Twydi had sent about three hours earlier. Opening then reading it, Rairai learned that it was sent to a woman named Felity. Twydi was confirming their meeting at a restaurant for tomorrow. Unfortunately, this was the last message so it didn't explain where Twydi was now or why he would go somewhere today without his infolio. The only appointment listed on his calendar for this evening was the meeting he was supposed to have with Rairai.

Outside, the hail continued hitting the windows and was now piling up on the balcony. Twydi, wherever he was, certainly wouldn't be returning home tonight, and since Rairai couldn't leave, he decided to make himself comfortable. As he headed back towards the bedroom, he heard the hail suddenly stop. This was then immediately followed by the sound of torrential rain.

When he reached the room, Rairai could see things outside flying past the large window…tree branches…debris…even some balcony loungers. He was glad not to have been caught in this unexpected tempest.

Walking over to the messy bed, he straightened out the blanket before sitting down. After kicking off his shoes, he began to look through his own infolio just in case Twydi had managed to get a message through. There was no message, but the new numbers for Heaven Sent were just in and they were even better than anticipated. He could only think about how pleased Twydi would be when he saw them. He then set down the infolio on the side table and laid back on the bed. Of course, Twydi had splurged on the most expensive Comfolax-Plush-Plush pillow, and Rairai's head sunk down into its luxurious softness. He stared at the ceiling for a short while as he felt himself begin to fall asleep. It had been such a busy week and a long, frustrating day.

That night, Rairai did not sleep peacefully. He dreamt of strange disturbing murmurings…things in the darkness he could not make out…things calling in distress…things muffled…straining to be understood. Three times he woke to the crashing sounds of the terrible storm outside, then each time fell back into unsettled slumber. He would not know the full extent of the hurricane until the next morning.

CHAPTER 12

Atira stood on the balcony and looked out over the neighbourhood. The ground was strewn with broken branches and other things the storm winds had claimed as their own. The chaotic sight was in stark contrast to the stillness and quiet of the beautiful sunny morning. Seeing the mess, Atira found herself worrying about the ones who may not have had adequate shelter. Did they all manage to find refuge? She was so glad it was over and hoped she would not have to go that far again. Looking at the blue sky, she reassured herself that it was a necessary act of purification and not one of violence.

Despite the fierceness of the storm, Atira had enjoyed a good sleep full of many dreams. Only once did she dream of *him*...only briefly...and without ever actually seeing him. She wished she did not dream of him at all, but knew she had to be thankful for small mercies. *It's my fault for holding on. I should have let go before it got this far. My Naomh warned me about clinging to things in this world. This is the risk of being so hungry in a world full of poisonous fruit.*

As she was just about to turn and go inside to begin her day's work, she suddenly spotted three hovercrafts coming down the street. Atira watched as they came to a stop in front of her house. Two were of the kind belonging to wealthy Lessers. They were smaller and not as elaborately designed as the ones the Noblatjs used. The ostentatious third was clearly that of a Noblatj.

The doors opened on the first vehicle and out popped a Lesser along with the maid she had allowed to leave. From the second vehicle, appeared two more Lessers. All four of them walked over and stood at attention outside the larger decorative third hover-craft. When the Noblatj stepped out, they all bowed their heads in reverence.

The Noblatj, his shiny green hair tied in a twist knot upon his head, said something to the group, causing the maid to turn and point up at Atira. It was obvious what they had come about. They had come to try and remove her from her house. The maid must have informed the relatives, and they in turn made a deal with the Noblatj. As they brought no police with them, it was clear that they had chosen not to inform the authorities. If they had, the house would have been confiscated and simply passed on to a Noblatj who was a benefactor of the Police Head. The relatives would have been left with nothing. By doing it this way, that green-haired Noblatj could quietly take possession of the property then compensate the relatives for their silence and co-operation. Such back-door deals were commonplace on this planet. Atira was just glad they had decided to do it this way. It made things less complicated for her.

She watched as they began to make their way up the front walk-way. Without giving it a second thought, she removed her quan-tum-eraser from her pocket and, in an instant, all five people were disintegrated. Next, she pointed it at the hovercrafts to eliminate that evidence, but before she activated it, a moment of doubt creeped in and she found herself pausing to survey the street. Were there any witnesses about? As wealthy Lessers do not normally wake until after midday she already knew there was almost no chance anyone would see, and had anyone been looking, she would have sensed their presence long before she had used her weapon. This loss of trust in her own instincts was a problem. If only she had not mind-merged with *him*, it would not be such a struggle. The flaws from his mind were now causing too much unnecessary doubt in her own.

Quickly shaking it off, she activated the quantum-eraser once again and the hovercrafts were gone. Everything was now still and quiet, and there was no sign of anyone having ever been outside her house.

CHAPTER 13

"NO!" screamed Rairai bolting upright in the bed. For a moment, he could not remember where he was, but then, slowly, he began to recognize the familiar things in the room. Yes, Twydi's place. I'm at Twydi's place. He then remembered the horrible storm the night before, and half expecting it to still be going on, he looked over at the window. A sense of relief washed over him to see the sky was now perfectly clear and the sun was shining.

It had been a terrible night for him...strange, restless and uncomfortable. He knew he had dreams, but he couldn't remember anything about them. He thought that, considering the unsettled feelings those dreams had left behind, perhaps this was a good thing.

Moving to the edge of the bed, Rairai grabbed his infolio from the side table. When he opened it, he was relieved to see a notice that the storm lock-down had now been lifted. It was okay to go outside without the fear of a fine or incarceration.

Placing the infolio back on the table, he then stood up and stretched his arms wide. Rairai flinched at the little painful twinge in his neck. Tilting his head this way and that, he tried to loosen up the muscles, hoping that would help. It didn't. The little pain just wouldn't go away. For all the money, you spent on that high-end pillow, Twydi, it doesn't work very well.

But where was Twydi? Rairai was now beginning to worry again. Stop worrying! There's nothing to be concerned about. It's just the same old Twydi. Impatient, incorrigible, Twydi. Probably he was in such a hurry to see that girl or some other girl, that he forgot his infolio. That's where he is now. Curled up with some honey-snap, while I'm here worrying and getting neck pain from his ridiculous over-priced pillow.

Rairai then remembered the unsigned documents and his uneasiness worsened. Lofty Bitterridge would not be happy the deadline was missed. He could even take it as a personal insult. There was nothing riskier than to anger a Noblatj and there were all kinds of ways they could be punished for such a transgression. Twydi knew this, so why was he being so irresponsible?

There were many days when Rairai had felt tempted to make his life easier by ending his partnership with Twydi, but these were always only passing thoughts. The truth was that they had been friends for a long time, and despite Twydi's frustratingly unreliable ways, there remained a deep and abiding loyalty between them.

Rairai walked over to the window and stared out at the sun-drenched world. In contrast to the perfectly clear sky above, was the complete mess below. Furniture from balconies, branches from trees and debris of all sort covered the ground. In the distance, he noticed a Noblatj administration building with its top floor completely sheared off. This had been quite a storm.

Turning back to the room, he then thought again about Twydi and found himself getting angry. Twydi, where the hell are you! You're making this difficult for both of us! Why do I always have to bear the brunt of your mistakes!

He considered for a moment, whether he should resume the search for his partner, but then decided it would be more prudent not to waste anymore time and, instead, go immediately to Lofty Bitterridge to beg for forgiveness. The longer he avoided doing this, the more time there was for the Noblatj's anger to grow and the worse the punishment would be. Rairai then headed into the bathroom to freshen up.

As he stared at his reflection in the mirror, the dark bags under his tired eyes mocked him with suggestions of impending mortality. "Get out of here!" he exclaimed aloud as if just saying that would make them shrink and disappear. He then ran his fingers through his dishevelled hair and looked down at his wrinkled clothing. What a mess! I need a full clean…clothes and all.

He opened the door to the aural-waves shower and was just about to step inside when he stopped cold. "What is that!" Rairai felt a chill run down his spine. On floor of the shower was a dark stain. He squatted to get a better look at it, hoping it wasn't what he thought. A closer inspection gave him no reassurance. This was undoubtedly dried blood.

CHAPTER 14

A tira sat in front of the console and analyzed the data. The storm had not only destroyed strategic targets, but it had also helped to purify the energy of the planet. It made people more open and aware of their vulnerabilities…more thoughtful about many things. Now, she needed to work on the next step, sending a saraph-stream over some particularly difficult areas. The Noblatjs and wealthy Lessers were destroying all hope in those places and something had to be done to pause the destruction. The saraph-stream would affect their brains, causing a tendency towards miscalculations in areas of judgements that would normally serve Moloch. It would also, over time, hopefully help some of them to evolve, but the setting had to be just right. Too much would mean the end of everyone on the planet and too little would be of no use. She carefully set the level for the perfect balance.

Just as she finished sending the saraph-stream, she heard the front doorbell. Her first thought was that more people had found out about her and were arriving to try and claim the house. She reached into her pocket and ran her fingers over her quantum-eraser, hoping she was wrong. Atira derived no satisfaction from using her weapon. It was merely an unfortunate necessity. This world made many things necessary that she did not enjoy. She did not want to have to erase any more people, but she would have no choice if they got in the way of her mission.

From her console, she accessed the home monitoring system and was able to view a small group of Lessers standing at the front door. These were not like the others, however. They were not wealthy by any means. They were a rag-tag looking group made up of one man, two old women, one younger woman and three children. "What is it that you want?" Atira asked them through the intercom.

"Please Mistress, my name is Taqwi and these are my friends. We have fallen on hard times and have just barely survived the storm. We have no money to buy food. It has been two days since the little ones have eaten. Please have mercy upon us," pleaded the thin but strong looking man.

Atira stared into their faces and opened her mind to their intentions. She sensed they were not takers like so many others she had met on this planet. They would accept with gratitude anything she had to offer. It was the law of her world that you must help those who ask honestly for help and she knew these people were being honest about their need. Also, it was the storm that had increased their suffering, so it was her duty to help even if it possibly slowed the mission a little.

"How many of you are there?" she asked. "I see seven. Are there more?"

"Mistress, there are more, but not here," said the man. "I have only brought the neediest among us. These women are elderly. This woman is pregnant, and the three children have not eaten in two days. I'm worried for their health. Anything, no matter how small, would be greatly appreciated. We would not come to your door and ask if we were not so desperate."

"Wait there," said Atira. She then glanced once more at the saraph-stream data before heading downstairs.

CHAPTER 15

Rairai had changed his mind about going to see Lofty Bitterridge. He wanted to first find Twydi. The blood in the shower had unnerved him and he now needed to ensure his friend was alright before doing anything else. The message in Twydi's communication log indicated that he should be meeting a woman for brunch. As Rairai stood under the bright pink glowing sign of the Two Moons Bistro, he just hoped Twydi was in there…that silly cocky grin on his face…feasting without a care on some over-priced dish.

When Rairai entered the restaurant, he could not see Twydi, but he immediately spotted the woman who must be Felity. From her fashionable fan hairdo, tight syntho-plastic clothing and large remodelled breasts, he knew this had to be her. She's the only one here who would fit Twydi's type.

He walked up to the table and asked, "Felity?"

She smiled at him with the kind of well-practiced flirty smile that he knew would have hooked Twydi right away.

"Yes," she replied. "Did Twydi send you?" She looked him up and down, trying to assess whether he was wealthy enough to warrant her attention.

"No, he didn't. Actually, I'm looking for him and thought I might find him here. I have his infolio."

"Oh, that explains why he hasn't returned my messages," she said. "I've tried him so many times, wondering where he could be. Although I haven't known him long, he's always been on time for our dates. This is unusual for him. Are you by any chance Rairai?"

"Yes, I am."

She smiled eagerly and said, "He's mentioned you many times. You're his business partner, right? He never mentioned that you were so handsome."

Rairai wanted to get back to the topic of Twydi. He sat down in the chair across from the table. "Do you have any idea where Twydi might have gone? I've checked every place I know."

Felity thought about it for a moment and then said, "The last time I spoke with him, he did say something about meeting up with some Noblatj. I forget the name."

"Was it Lofty Bitterridge?" asked Rairai.

"Yes!" she replied. "That was it. Apparently, he's a very important Noblatj of the highest standing, so Twydi told me."

"Did he say where or when this meeting was to take place?"

"No…well, not exactly. All I know is that he was very excited about the meeting. He said something about a big opportunity. Bigger even than what he had now. He said he'd be rolling in money, and that he'd buy me something really nice," she said with a giggle.

Rairai thought for a moment. Twydi had not mentioned anything about a meeting with Lofty Bitterridge to him. Why would he not do that? They had always been equal partners and up front with each other…well mostly. Could all this success have gone to Twydi's head and made him greedy to the point where he would cut out his old friend? It was possible. Twydi was the kind of man who dreamed of excess. He could be easily tempted in a moment of selfishness… at least temporarily.

Rairai stood up. "If you do see him, could you let him know that I have his infolio, and that he needs to get in touch with me as soon as possible."

"Sure," smiled Felity. "Maybe you should give me your symbol just in case I need to get in touch with you."

Rairai knew that if he gave her his symbol, he'd never get rid of her. When Twydi tired of her, and he always did, she'd start calling him. "I have your symbol in Twydi's infolio and will get in touch if I need to," he said.

"You do that," she replied, tilting her fan head seductively.

Rairai got up and left. Outside the restaurant, he stopped to check his infolio for any new messages. He also checked Twydi's, but there was nothing new to indicate where his partner might be. At that point, he could think of only one other place to look for a possible clue. He knew it would be awkward asking Lofty Bitterridge about Twydi. It was not a Lesser's place to ever ask questions of a Noblatj, but he would have to do it. He'd just have to approach it as delicately as possible.

CHAPTER 16

A tira removed the pan from the sonic-cooker. She then placed the second helping of steaming mabba bread in front of the children, making them squeal with delight. They had never seen so much food before. It warmed her heart to see these little ones, who had appeared so lost and forlorn when they had arrived at her door, now sparkling with happiness. She also noticed how, despite their hunger, they never grabbed for themselves alone, but instead carefully divided everything into equal portions. There was indeed something in this world worth saving.

"You have been so kind to us, Mistress," said Taqwi. "How can we possibly thank you?" Taqwi would have been grateful had someone just given them a little money for food. To be invited into this woman's house and to eat at her table was unbelievable. That morning it was only out of sheer desperation that he had decided to take the neediest of his group in search of immediate charity. Usually homeless Lessers would not be allowed to enter such a neighborhood, but when he saw that the gates were open, he thought it was a chance worth taking.

"Do you require anything more to eat?" asked Atira, thinking that she should get back upstairs to return to work. There was so much to do and so little time.

Taqwi hesitated then said, "You've been so generous, and I hate to ask, but for the children, if you have any extra blankets or clothes, it would be so appreciated? We would be so grateful for anything you can spare. Our camp is in the hills just outside of this neighborhood, and it gets very cold at night. What little shelter there was has been almost completely destroyed."

"How many are you?" Atira asked.

"Including everyone here, there are twenty."

Atira thought about it and then said, "This floor will accommodate twenty. I will take the upstairs, but you may stay here."

Taqwi couldn't believe his ears. "Here?" he asked. "You are inviting us to live here with you?"

"Yes," she replied. "There are many rooms. This floor should accommodate you all."

"But Mistress, what of your family? Will they object to finding us here? We are very poor Lessers." Taqwi was now beginning to worry that there was something wrong with this woman's mind. If he accepted her offer and she was not mentally sound, her family would certainly return and have them all arrested for theft. Even the little ones would be sent away to prison.

"Do not address me as Mistress," she replied. "My name is Atira. I am alone here. I am a part of no family and it's my choice that you may have this floor to live. It's dry and warm, and there is plenty of food. There are also many closets full of all sorts of clothes. What doesn't fit, you may alter."

Taqwi still couldn't believe it. "But as I said, we are very poor Lessers with nothing. How will we repay you?"

Atira thought about it. It was important not to leave them feeling like they owed her as these were obviously people who believed in fair exchange. She must respect their ways. "I will be very busy with my work…too busy to do the ordinary things that need to be done around here. If you could replenish the food-producer and keep the house and garden tidy, that is enough. You will also be my guardians to ensure that no one trespasses or disturbs my work. Can you do these things?"

Taqwi was not sure what to say. The entire thing was so strange.

Why would a wealthy Lesser be so kind to them and what sort of work did she do that was so important? If he accepted, would he be taking the group into a dangerous situation? She certainly didn't seem dangerous. In fact, it was just the opposite. There was something about her that made him feel calm and reassured. He noticed the children felt it too. There was certainly an ingenuous air about her, and they did so desperately need all she was offering. "Yes," Taqwi said decidedly. "We will do that for you and more. All you need is to ask, and we will provide as best we can. I still cannot believe your generosity to us. If I may ask, what kind of Lesser are you?"

Atira did not want to lie to him, but she also did not want him to know the truth, so she told him, "Where I come from we are taught that how you treat those in need is how you treat yourself. When I feed you, I feed myself. When I clothe you, I clothe myself. That is all you need to know."

"That is so beautiful!" exclaimed one of the elderly women who had been listening.

"Where you come from must be a wonderful place," said Taqwi, wondering where on this planet such a community would exist, but feeling like he should not push it any further...at least for now.

"Yes, it is," replied Atira. "It is a wonderful place, and I miss it very much."

CHAPTER 17

Rairai looked over at the puffy-faced receptionist busily working at her console. He had been waiting almost three hours to see Bitterridge. Three times he had approached her and asked how much longer, and three times she told him, "Lofty Bitterridge is an extremely busy Noblatj and will get to you as soon as it is your turn. A good Lesser is a patient Lesser." He began to wonder if he was being punished for the late documents.

Taking out his infolio, Rairai checked once again for any message from Twydi. This was something he had done constantly since he arrived. There was still nothing. He began to tap his foot nervously against the floor.

Finally, the receptionist looked over at him and chirped, "He'll see you now Mr. Swyer."

The doors to the office area slid open and Rairai leapt up. He then hurried down the waterfall hallway, barely noticing that the water had turned to black and the little fish were now a ghostly silver.

When he reached the ram-head doors, he pressed the buzzer. There was a brief moment of waiting, which seemed too long for Rairai, but then the doors slid open. He quickly stepped inside.

"Rairai!" exclaimed Lofty Bitterridge as he walked over to him. It surprised Rairai that Lofty Bitterridge should immediately address him in such a casual and friendly tone, and then stand so close. This was not normal protocol between Noblatjs and Lessers, and not a behavior he had exhibited before. It was especially strange in light of the fact that Bitterridge must know that some documents were overdue. Noblatjs were sticklers for promptness and certainly not the forgiving type when things were late.

"Lofty Bitterridge," Rairai replied, bowing his head.

"I was told you were eager to speak with me. The numbers are looking good…very good, so I know you are not here to discuss that. What is your concern?" he asked, tucking his long white hair behind his large pale ear.

"It's about Twydi. I haven't been able to contact him. I have the documents that were due yesterday, but I've been unable to get his mark to process them. I am so sorry about this, Lofty Bitterridge. I am truly sorry. As you know, it's not like Twydi to miss important deadlines. May I ask, did he say anything to you? Do you have any idea where he might be?"

"Me?" laughed Lofty Bitterridge. "Why would I know where he is? I have better things to do than to keep track of a Lesser."

"No, of course…of course you do. I apologize if I offended you," said Rairai. "It's simply that I cannot move forward without him. I thought that perhaps he may have come by to see you."

Lofty Bitterridge turned, walked over to his desk and sat down. "I have not seen him," he said. "Twydi has never been very reliable. He likely has taken a shuttle-ship to some secluded destination and is enjoying himself in the arms of some gigi-girl…maybe more than one." He then laughed heartily, boldly flashing his neon blue teeth.

"Yes, I know that Twydi has always been one to enjoy the pleasures in life," replied Rairai, "but I assure you, he does take our business very seriously. It isn't like him to just go missing when he knows there are things that need to be done…contracts to sign off on."

"Oh, never mind," said Lofty Bitterridge, with a casual wave of his arm. "As the Noblatj investor, I hereby give you permission to authorize documents without him for now. I'm certain he will show up, but in the meantime, we must keep things moving, mustn't we?"

"I...I suppose," replied Rairai.

"So, until Twydi gets tired of those women and returns, I suggest we carry on. If you have any other concerns, please feel free to come and see me. Open communication is something I believe is necessary to running a good business, and for good relations between Lessers and Noblatjs. Wouldn't you agree?"

"Yes...yes, it is," said Rairai, now worried more than ever and not knowing what else to say.

"Is there any other problem you need to bring to my attention?"

"No. No, Lofty Bitterridge. That is all."

"Very well. I don't mean to cut our meeting short, but I have an important function I must get to. And remember, if you have any concerns bring them to me immediately. That is what I am here for...to provide you with the guidance and the wisdom of Noblatjs."

Rairai bowed his head and said, "Thank you, Lofty Bitterridge." He then turned and left the room. As he walked alone down the long hallway, with its streaming black water and silver fish, he couldn't help thinking that something was not right. Felity said Twydi was supposed to meet with Bitterridge, but Bitterridge didn't mention anything about that. Was he being quiet about it because it is a business secret between him and Twydi, or is there something more to it? Rairai wasn't sure what to think. All he knew was that he had to find his friend.

CHAPTER 18

A s she sat at her console finishing up her most recent calculations, Atira heard the shouting and laughter of the children
downstairs. She knew they had just finished their afternoon snack
and now, full of energy, would be headed outside to play. It was the
same everyday, and she had come to depend on the sounds of their
schedule to help keep track of her own time.

In the beginning, she did have some concern that these people
could interfere with her mission. They might disturb her work or
bring unwanted attention to the house. But because it was part of
her commitment to the planet and to her code, she opened her
house to them anyway. As it turned out, this was indeed the right
decision. Not only were they not slowing down the mission, but
they were proving essential to it. They were taking good care of the
house along with her day to day needs, allowing her to focus entirely
on her work. She felt grateful to them.

Gently placing her fingers on the console, she entered in an
experimental equation and hoped it would give the result she was
looking for. Aligning the energies of this planet was complicated,
and equations had to be tested in smaller situations before they
could be deployed in larger ones. As she waited for the outcome of
her experiment, she suddenly felt a presence in the room with her.

Turning around, Atira saw that a small child had wandered upstairs and was now silently standing in the doorway. The girl had a tiny guilty smile on her face knowing that she was doing something she had been explicitly told not to do.

"Hello," Atira said to the little girl, not feeling angry at the disobedience of the child, but at that moment feeling glad of the company. It was easy to get lonely sitting at the console for so long.

Realizing she would not be chastised for coming upstairs, the child now moved a little further into the room.

"What is your name?" Atira asked.

"Meebelle," the little girl replied softly.

Atira looked back at her console. The results had now come through and indicated the trial was a success. This meant she could now carry through with her next project. "Come here Meebelle," she said. "And I will show you something."

Meebelle walked over to Atira and obediently stood by her chair.

"Do you see this?" asked Atira as she pointed to an image on her holographic screen. It was the visual of a large dam that sat above an important Noblatj office complex.

Meebelle quietly nodded.

"Do you know what it is?" Atira asked of her, and again Meebelle nodded.

Atira knew she didn't really comprehend what she was seeing, but that didn't matter. One day she would remember and understand. "This big bad wall, you see here, holds back all the good water, Meebelle," she told her. "But the good water must be set free. The good water is cleansing…purifying. This bad wall holds it back so that it cannot clean away the dirt. It also keeps the water from very thirsty people. This isn't good. We need to fix this."

"We need fix this," repeated Meebelle happily.

"Should we take down the big bad wall and set the good water free?" asked Atira. "Should we let it wash over everything? Make everything clean again?"

"Yes!" exclaimed Meebelle, excitedly.

"Do you see this little button? The blue one? This is a magic button that will make it all happen. Would you like to push it?"

"Now?" asked Meebelle, excited at the prospect of helping the important lady upstairs.

"Yes, now," replied Atira. "Take down the wall, now."

Meebelle let her tiny finger hover over the icon for a moment and then, with exaggerated gusto, pressed down upon it.

"Eeeee!" she squealed with delight as she watched the dam explode and the water burst through.

"Thank you, Meebelle,' said Atira. "The land will now be washed clean and the thirsty people will drink."

CHAPTER 19

Rairai stood outside of the front doors of the Bitterridge Building and thought about what he should do next. Even though he had an uncomfortable feeling that Lofty Bitterridge might know something about Twydi's disappearance, he also knew he couldn't press him any further. To ask again would be to overstep his mark and could easily get him thrown out of the company or even jailed if the Noblatj decided it was warranted. He had to search for more clues elsewhere.

It suddenly occurred to him that there was one place he hadn't yet checked…the Health Station. What if Twydi had some sort of accident and had gone there for help. It would certainly explain the blood in the shower and how Twydi might have been in such a hurry as to forget his infolio. Perhaps his feeling about Bitterridge was wrong after all and there was a perfectly innocent explanation.

When he arrived at the Station, it was not very busy. Rairai checked the admission panel for Twydi's name, but it wasn't listed. He then thought about how, without his infolio, Twydi would have to be identified by the chip in his palm. But this was a problem because both he and Twydi were in the process of having their identities upgraded to Class A. For the new chip to work properly, it required a full month of having no chip to allow new cells to grow.

Otherwise, it could result in a shadow effect and interfere with the new identification codes. If he had come here and was unable to communicate, Twydi would have been admitted as an unknown Lesser. Rairai approached the service desk to inquire.

"Excuse me," he said to the receptionist who had her back to him.

"Hello, how may I help you," she happily chirped as she turned to face him.

Rairai was suddenly taken aback to see Lofty Bitterridge's receptionist staring at him from behind the desk. It took him a moment to realize that this was an entirely different woman who had simply purchased the same surgical package. "I'm searching for my friend," he explained. "He didn't return home last night, and I'm worried about him. He isn't on the admission list, but I thought maybe he was admitted as an unknown. He doesn't have his infolio with him and he is temporarily without an identification chip. He was being upgraded."

"Upgraded? Well good for him! Good to see us hardworking Lessers moving up in the world. There are so many lazy ones about. That kind bring us all down. Anyway, let's see if we can find your friend," she said, then began to enter data into her console. "There were several unknowns admitted yesterday, but I'm afraid all of them were dead or died shortly after being admitted."

Rairai had a sinking feeling in his stomach. "Were any of them wealthy Lessers…well dressed. My friend was a very nice dresser."

The attendant laughed. "If that were the case, he would not have been labelled as an 'unknown'. No, it appears they were all vagabond Lessers. At least they were all listed as such. If the doctors had noticed any that were well-dressed, they would have been listed as a 'yet to be identified VIP corpse'. My list shows they were all just unknown Lessers."

Rairai paused to think about what he should do next. I can't leave without being certain he's not here. What if…what if they made a mistake? What if the doctor didn't notice his clothes or there was some sort of mix-up? "Could I see the bodies to ensure that there has been no mistake?" he asked.

"I assure you, sir, that we do not make mistakes here. We are very thorough. However, if it will give you peace of mind, just go through that door on your right, down the stairs, down the hall, and to the bio-matter storage area. There you will find an attendant by the name of Frizz. Explain to him that Yerta sent you for an identification search."

"Thank you," said Rairai who then walked to the door as directed. When he opened it, he could see the walls inside the stairwell were dirty and scratched, a stark contrast to the immaculate area of the upper floor. As he descended the stairs, he felt the air getting considerably colder. It made him shiver.

The hallway at the bottom was long, narrow and dimly lit. He warily made his way to a door with the words BIOMATTER STORAGE in glow-paint letters. As it didn't really seem necessary to knock, he simply pushed open the old-fashioned latch and walked in.

"Well, a visitor!" happily exclaimed an older white-haired man wearing a standard medical worker's protective silver jump-suit and standing behind a console. "The name is Frizz. How may I help you today, sir?" he asked cheerily as he closed the panel he had been viewing.

At first, Rairai wondered why this man would be so delighted to see him but then realized that he likely spent most days without seeing very many living people. "Yerta sent me for an identification search," he said.

"Oh Yerta," smiled the man. "I knew that woman three faces ago. Back then we had a little thing, you know. But not now. Now she thinks she's too good for me. Anyway, you didn't come here to listen to that sordid story. On to the identification search…what are you looking for…woman, man, child?"

"A man," said Rairai. "My friend went missing yesterday. He would have been well-dressed. His hair is brown. His eyes are blue. Is there someone here matching this description? He would have been brought in last night or perhaps today."

"Let me think," said Frizz. "We had five brought in. They all have brown hair. That's common. I didn't check the color of their eyes, although I believe one doesn't have any eyes at all. By the time I get them, their clothes are already gone so I can't help with that. Also, if he were robbed, his clothes could have been stolen or even switched. It's happened before. He didn't have an identification chip?"

"No, he was in the process of receiving an upgrade."

"An upgrade? How impressive! Yerta would be impressed by a man like that."

"Can I see them...the bodies," Rairai asked nervously.

"Of course," exclaimed Frizz. "Right this way."

Rairai followed him into an adjoining room. It was even colder than the previous one and he found himself shivering again. There was a console on his right and directly across was a large shiny metal wall with a circular opening about waist high.

Frizz went over to the console and brought up a panel. "Now, how old was your friend?" he asked. "That will help us narrow it down."

"Twydi was...is forty-three," Rairai answered. "He's had a little face-work done so he might look younger than that."

"That's okay. We determine the age by molecular analysis not by the face. Faces are deceiving. Just look at Yerta out there. You don't even want to know how old she is," Frizz said with a laugh.

There was an odd humming noise as he entered in the data. This was obviously not the most up to date equipment. "There are two here who are in the range of forty-three years of age," said Frizz. "I'll bring them up. Don't ask me where they found them as we don't collect that kind of data. After all they are only unknown Lessers. Now, go stand on the yellow circle over there and face the wall."

Rairai walked over, stood in the yellow circle and faced the metal wall.

"No," said Frizz, "not that wall, the white one."

Rairai turned and faced the white wall so that the metal wall was to his left side.

"In a moment, the body will slide out in front of you and you'll be able to view it," Frizz explained. "Take your time and remember not to touch it. Now, just as a warning, they can be quite shocking to look at, so try not to faint or get sick. We really should have them all in an image-database, but so few people come looking that they deemed it an unnecessary expenditure. Cost-savings and all. Are you ready?"

"Yes," replied Rairai even though he didn't feel ready.

He then watched as a metal table with a body slowly slid out of the opening and stopped right in front of him. He knew before even looking at the face that it wasn't Twydi. The feet were severely calloused. Those were the feet of a homeless Lesser. His eyes traveled up the gaunt body to the dead man's gray-mottled face. He then quickly looked away. "It's not him," he said.

"That's good news," replied Frizz who pushed the button on his console to make the body disappear back into the wall. "The next one is coming. Are you ready?"

Rairai braced himself as a metal table once again slid out of the opening with another body. Again, the first thing Rairai noticed were the feet. Although dirty and scratched, they did not seem hard and calloused like those of the other body. He felt a sinking feeling in his stomach. Mustering up his courage, he then looked at the face. It was severely bruised, one of the eyes was swollen shut and the skin was deathly grey in color, but there was no mistaking it. He knew that face. "Oh Twydi!" he gasped, grabbing hold of the metal table as his knees buckled beneath him.

CHAPTER 20

As Atira walked down the street, she noticed something different in the air. Each person she passed seemed just a little unsettled…less certain about the world. They were beginning to sense the dislodging that was now taking place. Dislodging is always essential in creating renewal and banishing Moloch. The fact that people were experiencing discomfort was a good sign.

She turned down a narrow lane and stood in front of a non-descript steel door. This is it. I will find what I need here.

Taking her decoder from her pocket, she waved it across the door, causing the locking mechanism to release and the door to slide open. She then cautiously peered inside. Relieved to see no one about, she quietly slipped in, closing the door behind her.

Inside, she could see that the walls were a standard worker grey. Although she already had an idea about where she needed to go, the color reassured her that this was the right place and that she had entered through the correct door. Any of the heavily guarded areas used by the Noblatjs would be decorated in the bright colors they believed gave them power. Noblatjs were very superstitious that way.

Atira knew that she would have to make her way into the upper well-protected floors if she were to find what she had come for. Taking out her geo-locator, she quickly assessed the layout of the building. There was a large open area with many small rooms and compartments just down the hall and to her left. She knew this to be a workers' preparation area where the Lessers would get their uniforms and store their personal items.

She cautiously made her way down the long grey corridor. When she reached the prep-area she carefully looked around to ensure it was empty. There was no sign of anyone, and the changing areas and aural-waves showers were unoccupied. She had timed it correctly.

At the far end of the room was a large bio-uniform dispenser. Atira walked over to the machine and studied the controls. She could see it operated by a combination of cranial reader and DNA recognition. Each worker would be required to place their head inside and then spit into the machine for identification. After their identity was confirmed, the machine would then dispense a fresh bio-uniform to be worn for the day. It was a more sophisticated security device than the palm chip reader, but because of the enormous cost, it was only used in high level buildings such as this one.

For Atira, it was actually a very simple machine that could easily be by-passed with an ordinary sonic tool. Before leaving for this planet, she had this handy little universal tool built into the nail of the smallest finger on her left hand. Reaching her hand inside of the machine, she opened the sonic tool and forced it into the cranial scanner where she gave it a quick right then a firm left twist. The machine immediately issued her a Level A-1 uniform. This garment was a shiny black long-sleeved self-closing smock worn over regular clothing. She quickly put it on and headed out to where her geo-locator indicated a cyber-lift would be.

When she reached the cyber-lift, the door opened, and she was surprised to come face to face with a worker who was also wearing a Level A-1 uniform. He looked her over suspiciously. "What project are you assigned to?" he bluntly asked. "I've not seen you here before."

"It's a new one," Atira replied. "It involves the regeneration of the Noblatjs skin cells. As you know, the bleaching process they enjoy is slowly breaking down cellular structure. I am working on a formula that will stop and reverse this problem. Previously I was at

Building 203 but have been reassigned here."

The worker smiled, "Yes, that is a problem for our great Noblatjs. Good to have you with us."

It was then that Atira realized the man had not been worried she was an intruder, but instead, was suspicious she was there to take his coveted position as a Level A-1 worker. She was glad of that. The degree of selfishness and paranoia that Moloch had dispersed across this planet made the aliens weak and distracted. That was always to her advantage.

As soon as the worker stepped out, Atira entered the cyber-lift and tapped the icon for the top floor.

CHAPTER 21

Rairai burst into the reception area. "I need to see Lofty Bitter-ridge right now!" he shouted.

The receptionist backed away as she clicked the small button near her console screen. Almost immediately, two large security guards burst into the room and stood on either side of Rairai.

"I'm sorry," he apologized, realizing he was probably going to be thrown out of the building or even worse. Making a scene in a Noblatj's space was a grave offense. He lowered his voice and said, "I'm just upset. Something horrible has happened and I must speak with Lofty Bitterridge, please!"

"His Loftiness is not taking appointments today," said the receptionist, firmly.

"You don't understand," pleaded Rairai, trying his best to keep his emotions under control. "Something terrible has happened. I must speak with him. It's urgent!"

"I can leave a message for him, but as I said, he is not seeing anyone today. Perhaps tomorrow."

Rairai felt dizzy. He could feel the two men now moving closer on either side of him. "Please," he tried once again.

The receptionist smiled her best fake puffy-faced smile. "If I could do anything for you, you know I would, Mr. Swyer, but the

Noblatjs know best. We must all be patient believing that they will take care of everything. As I said, your message will be the first one he will see tomorrow. You will simply have to wait until then."

Rairai took two steps back then stopped and stared at the door to the waterfall hallway. For a moment, he thought about charging through to get to Bitterridge, but his common sense told him that, even if by chance he reached the door, that was as far as he was going to get. Also, just attempting such a thing would certainly get him thrown into prison, and perhaps even a death sentence. So instead, he composed himself as best he could and said, "I'm sorry. Please forgive me. A tragedy has made me foolish and impulsive. As you instruct, I will wait for Lofty Bitterridge to contact me. Please accept my apology. I will leave now." Without looking at the security guards, he then turned, and headed outside.

On the street, Rairai paused for a moment to think. He needed to find out for certain whether or not Twydi had gone to see Lofty Bitterridge, but how? There were many security cameras mounted on the Bitterridge Building, but knew he'd never be allowed to access the footage. For any Lesser to ask for such a thing could be a considered a crime against the Noblatjs. So instead, he walked down the street in the direction of the Lesser hovercraft station to try and retrace Twydi's possible steps.

About a block down he saw a kiosk with a jupa-juice vendor. He knew these small vendors always had security cameras to deter the homeless Lessers from a grab-and-run. If he could examine this man's data-pin, he might be able to find something there. "Hello," he said to the man behind the counter, "I wonder if you could help me. Two days ago, I was robbed by a homeless Lesser. I believe that he ran by this way. The authorities have not been able to find him, but I thought, if I had a picture of him, it could put him in prison. And I was thinking, he just might have been caught by your security camera. This is the second time I have been jumped by one of these ruffians and am willing to pay good money for any evidence that may help to apprehend him."

"Say no more," said the vendor. "Something has to be done about these filthy animals. They feel they are entitled to what others have worked so hard for." He reached up to his camera and pulled out the data-pin. "Here, take it, and I hope you find him. The faster they lock those animals up the better."

Rairai took the pin in his hand. "Thank you," he said. "Are you sure I can't pay you."

"No. It's no problem. I have so many data-pins. My brother gets them for me. He works at the factory where they make them…slips a few in his pockets. You know…" the man said with a wink.

"Well, thank you…and your brother. I'll be sure to let you know if they find him."

"Good! Get them all off the street, I say. Lock those filthy thieves up!"

"Thanks again," said Rairai as he walked away, the data-pin tucked securely in his pocket. He only hoped it would reveal something.

CHAPTER 22

The doors of the cyber-lift opened and Atira stepped out into the luxuriously decorated hallway. She was immediately met by a tall muscular guard with a security infolio in his hand.

"Reason for your presence," he demanded as he scanned her uniform for an identifying signature.

Atira didn't want to have to erase him. He was, after all, just an ordinary Lesser trying to do his job. The eraser was only to be used when absolutely necessary. Her Naomh had made that very clear. "I am here to report on project 984," she told him.

"Project 984? I've never heard of that," he began to scroll through his infolio.

"It's a new classified project for the personal and private needs of the Noblatjs." Atira knew this was an acceptable answer as it was not unusual for such a project to be secret enough not to be listed. The Noblatjs were adamant about privacy, especially when it came to their vanity.

The guard looked her over. Her bio-uniform had checked out, but she didn't have any of the tell-tale signs of facial modification that were so popular among Level A-1 workers. "You will have to get an authorized pass to access this floor," he said, deciding to go with the higher-level security protocols.

Atira sighed to know that the man had now given her no choice. It was one of the most unpleasant aspects of her mission. "I see," she replied then reached into her sleeve and took out her quantum-eraser. Before he even knew what was happening, the guard was gone. The way was now clear.

Checking her geo-locator, she could see that what she was looking for was close by. Walking down the bright blue corridor, she came to an unmarked door, barely visible given it was the same color as the wall. When she tried to open it, she discovered it was locked. A quick wave of her decoder and it easily slid open.

There was no one inside the room as the helia-powered generator did not require constant supervision. It worked autonomously, supplying Noblatj neighborhoods with energy for their homes and hovercrafts. It did sometimes require adjustments to increase or decrease output, but that was done by the Noblatjs themselves, and happened very rarely. She quickly stepped inside, sliding the door shut behind her.

Like all the rooms used by Noblatjs, this one was lavishly decorated. Atira walked across the glowing multi-colored floor tiles to the large wall console. There, she searched for the hidden panel that would give her access to the inner workings of the generator. Running her hands over the wall, she tried to feel for the faint outline of its square shape. Finding it, she pressed her hand into the center, and it popped open, revealing a mess of wires, tubes and sonic transmitters. Beneath all this, tucked in at the back, was the green glowing rod she had come for...the helia-rod!

Atira reached inside and quickly by-passed the energy flow wires to a secondary back-up generator. The generator would be able to power the machine for several hours which was more than enough time for her to get what she needed and leave. Then, as she carefully detached the helia-rod, she heard the door slide open and immediately shut behind her.

"Who are you?!"

Atira turned to see a Noblatj had entered the room. His long black metallic hair framed his angry ghostly white face.

"What are you doing here and what are you doing with that?!"

he barked as he pointed at the helia-rod in her hand. Had he felt threatened, he would have called for security right away, but Atira looked small and he had enjoyed killing much larger Lessers before. There was no doubt in his mind he could easily kill her also.

As Atira set down the helia-rod on a nearby counter, the Noblatj suddenly rushed her, but before he could place even one hand upon her, she grabbed him by the throat, spun him around and pinned him up against the wall. For a moment, he was simply stunned by her surprising strength, but then he began to desperately claw at her hands as he sputtered and gasped for air.

Atira looked deep into his eyes saw the deadness of Moloch swirling like fetid pools within those black pupils. The sight of it made her feel sick and disgusted, and she knew this Noblatj was so deeply infected he could not be eliminated silently. It required the power of words. She had to make this man fully aware of what was happening and why. This way the message would resound across the universe and hit Moloch directly with harsh waves of truth. Truth was unbearable to Moloch and would weaken him. "I will explain something to you," she calmly told the Noblatj. "Today you will no longer exist. You will no longer oppress the people of this planet. You will no longer steal or create violence or revel in death and destruction. In this moment, know that there is nothing worthy about you. You are empty...willfully empty." As she said this she reached into her pocket with her free hand. "You are about to be erased from this planet...from this universe. You will exist no more," she told him. "But before that happens, I want you to know that this monstrosity of a world you have helped to build is over. Although you will not live to see its destruction, you will die knowing that it is all over. You and all you have achieved are nothing. Do you hear me? Nothing! It will all be wiped away forever." She pressed the quantum-eraser against his terrified face and activated it. In an instant, he was gone.

Picking up the helia-rod and tucking it under her uniform, Atira then walked over to a small panel on the other side of the room. She opened it and using her sonic tool wiped clean all the buildings' security cameras. For her own protection and the protection of the refugees in her house, there could be no record of her ever having been there.

CHAPTER 23

Rairai replayed the footage on the data pin. It was not a perfect picture, but there was no doubt. That was Twydi walking by the jupa-juice stand. He knew it was him by his walk and that ridiculous flashy jacket. Twydi was so proud of that jacket. The day he bought it, he bragged to Rairai about how much it cost. "It's a one of a kind. An original. Noblatj quality. Of course, it's not too much to pay," he told him.

Rairai stared at the screen. The time and date indicated that it was the afternoon of the day before the great storm, and Twydi was definitely headed in the direction of the Bitterridge Building. Whether Bitterridge had something to do with Twydi's death, he still couldn't be certain. But now he did know that Bitterridge must have been lying about meeting with Twydi.

Rairai fast forwarded to the point where Twydi was passing by in the other direction and then paused it. There was his friend, still full of life, a far cry from the battered corpse he had seen at the Health Station. The time shown indicated that two hours had gone by since Twydi first passed the stand.

What happened? Rairai needed to know. He thought about how, if Twydi was going to meet with Bitterridge, why did he not mention it to him? Then again, Twydi was a wheeler-dealer. It would be just like him to have an idea for a new investment and then decide to run it by the Noblatj alone. Twydi always had all sorts of business dealings going on at once with most of them going nowhere. And he had, in the past, even associated with some rather shady characters. He was not above being secretive about his other schemes, but usually once they appeared to have any potential, he would come clean and share them with Rairai. Still, he had changed a lot since the Heaven Sent success.

What Rairai knew for sure is that, if Twydi was going to meet with Bitterridge, he would have had his infolio with him. He would not have left it behind in his apartment. Therefore, he must have made it home again. That's where it happened or at least that's from where he was taken. Besides the dried blood in the aural-waves shower, there was no other indication of foul play…no signs of struggle.

This could suggest that Twydi had not been murdered in his home but was taken somewhere else. The actual murder would have happened in another location. *Murdered*…Rairai shuddered at the word. *My friend was murdered.*

He then un-paused the data pin and watched as Twydi walked by the jupa-juice stand and out of sight. Part of him felt like replaying it just to watch him walk by again. He wanted to pretend that Twydi was still alive, but he knew this would only make him feel worse than he did already. *I need to talk with Bitterridge, regardless of the danger. And I know that even if I find out he had something to do with Twydi's death, there's nothing that can be done about it. The law is on the side of the Noblatjs not the Lessers. But I can't ignore it. Twydi was a good man…a good friend. Yes, he was confused about a lot of things, but at heart, he was a good man. I need to at least try and find out what happened to him. I owe him that much.*

CHAPTER 24

Atira was on the floor at the base of her console finishing up the necessary adaptations for the helia-rod installation. Although the rod was not completely compatible with her machine, she believed that she could make it work. It would take a little know-how and a lot of ingenuity, but it was possible. She had done similar adaptations on other planets with great success.

This is a common problem when building trans-dimensionally. It's simply impossible to work out perfect calculations for the energy source. Moving protons between dimensions results in continuously changing variables. It's very easy to be one or two power points off regardless of the care and skill put into it. Unfortunately, the problem can't be seen while working through dimensions. It's only after physically arriving on the alien world and using the console that one would realize an additional source of energy is needed for optimum performance. The helia-rod was the closest thing she could find to the solaplasm used on her own world and, in theory, it should work.

She adjusted the central input one more time before carefully picking up the glowing green helia-rod beside her. Slowly and with precision she clicked it into place. There was a sudden surge in energy causing the holographic screen above her to suddenly blast the room with a blinding light. Realizing that the entire thing was on the verge of exploding, she quickly installed a dampening ring to control output. Instantly, the screen returned to a more normal brightness.

Atira closed the panel, stood up and began to enter information into the console to test that it was working to specifications. She felt relieved to find no glitches of any significance. Overall, it now appeared to be operating more efficiently and effectively. She was relieved it was a success. Operating on the old system was slowing down her work and could have possibly jeopardized the mission.

The alien technology was now increasing the capacity of the console, making it able to accept more complicated calculations to build more tools. Atira entered some of her already proven equations into the machine, causing the holographic screen to suddenly become more vivid and displaying a much more detailed living-map of the planet. She started to explore the added features, zeroing in on highly specific targets. From her console, she could now see almost any place in the world as well as hear the conversations. As a test, she zoomed in on a Noblatj's home where she saw a maid fitting the Noblatj with a waist-cincher.

"Oww," shouted the Noblatj who then hit the woman across her head.

"I'm so sorry, Lofty Snople. Please forgive me," replied the maid.

Atira zoomed out again to examine the larger map. My work will move faster now, and it should be more accurate. With this new burst of energy, I will be able to accomplish things I was not able to accomplish before.

She scanned the map for the glowing red dots. These were the hotspots…the places where the Noblatjs had gathered to decide policy. When they came together like this, to form ideas that would increase their power and control, there was a natural buildup of Moloch's vacuity-force. This is what the console was picking up, and this is how she would begin to pick them off. She zoomed in on one of the dots and could see a group of Noblatjs sitting around one of their mirror-black sanctified meeting tables. They held the belief that these long rectangular tables crafted from the mosi tree would ensure success in their business dealings.

"It's a matter of getting rid of a few Lessers, that's all," said one, his bright pink hair piled high on top of his head.

"But what if someone notices. To get rid of one or two, yes, but such a large group at once? It would look too obvious and we can't afford to look obvious at this time."

"After all our planning and work, we can't afford not to follow through. There's huge profit in these mines and those Lessers will not remove themselves. They need to be eliminated and soon."

"But there's been talk of a revolution already. The Lessers do outnumber us. They breed like quinrats. We have to be careful not to raise suspicion."

"Ah, the talk of a revolution is only your paranoia. What kind of a Noblatj are you to fear Lessers? They wouldn't dare question our right to exterminate this group. We will go ahead with the plan tonight."

Atira knew there was no time to lose. Quickly entering in the necessary code, she then watched as, with a thunderous crack, the floor beneath the Noblatjs suddenly split open and the walls and ceiling came crashing in. They didn't even have a chance to cry out before they all disappeared beneath the rubble.

Staring at the lifeless dust cloud now on her panel, Atira waited for what would come next. Within mere seconds, a wave of life energy suddenly surged into the world and through her. This was the way of things. When a large part of Moloch is removed…when that dead part is cut out, it makes room for light and it is through light that life increases. *Life exists in pure desire as it waits on the edge of darkness, longing for beautiful light.* Her mission was to birth that light into existence through whatever means necessary. Her mission was to create more light to make room for the power of life.

CHAPTER 25

Rairai had waited two days for a call from Lofty Bitterridge but heard nothing. His patience had run out and he decided that regardless of the risk, he should return to the Bitterridge Building. Showing up in person would be his best chance at getting a meeting.

When he arrived, the receptionist did not even want to inform the Noblatj that he was there. "I have strict instructions that His Greatness is not to be disturbed today," she told him.

But Rairai would not accept this. Twydi was dead...murdered. He had to see Bitterridge. "I appreciate how busy such an important Noblatj as Lofty Bitterridge can be, but I am the man behind Heaven Sent," he said. "I am not simply just anyone off the street. I need to speak with him today and I'm willing to wait in this reception room for however long it takes." He then leaned himself against the wall across from her desk and stared directly at her.

The receptionist, looking very uncomfortable, entered some information into her console and then stared for a while at her panel. Eventually, she said, "Mr. Swyer, you will be given a few moments of Lofty Bitterridge's time, but only a few moments. Please go through."

Rairai went through the door and hurried down the hall. He noticed that the waterfall walls had either been turned off or were broken. Regardless, he didn't give it a second thought. There were more important things at hand.

Once inside the office, he boldly approached Lofty Bitterridge's desk. He knew he was thwarting protocol with this behavior, but he didn't care. If he was only to be given a moment to ask questions, there was no time for formalities.

Lofty Bitterridge was visibly annoyed by Rairai's audaciousness, but before he could say anything, Rairai blurted out, "Twydi is dead! He's been murdered!"

For a moment, Lofty Bitterridge went silent. He then asked, "Murdered? How do you know this?"

"I found his body. It was being stored as an unknown Lesser at the Health Station."

"Well," said Bitterridge. "That is an unfortunate thing."

"It was not unfortunate, it was murder!" retorted Rairai a little too sharply. "And I intend to find out who murdered him, but I need your help."

"And how am I to help?"

"You may have been the last one to see him. I broke into the locked messages in his infolio and it mentioned a tentative meeting with you. It might have had something to do with a project called Swan Song he had been working on. It was one I wasn't particularly interested in, already having my hands full with Heaven Sent," Rairai lied.

"Swan Song? A meeting with me?" Lofty Bitterridge stared past Rairai. "No such meeting occurred, and I've never heard of Swan Song before. I already made it clear to you that I have not seen him. The last time I saw Twydi was two weeks ago in the meeting with the three of us. I'm afraid I cannot help."

"Are you certain?" persisted Rairai.

Lofty Bitterridge now stared directly at Rairai with his piercing ice-blue eyes. "Let me make this clear. I do not know anything about the death of this Lesser…a Lesser known to associate with many questionable characters. It should be a surprise to no one that he has ended up dead. Such things happen to such people. Also, two Noblatjs have mysteriously gone missing which is of far greater importance. Now, your time is up, and you will respectfully thank me for granting you this audience. If you wish to contact me again, it will be regarding the company only. Twydi is a problem for the police, not for me. Do you understand?"

Rairai could see that he would get no more than this. He now felt certain that Lofty Bitterridge had something to do with it, but he had to be careful. The wrong step and he could meet the same fate as Twydi. "Thank you, Lofty Bitterridge," he said with a bow. "I am just grateful that you were able to see me at this busy time. I am so sorry if I offended you in anyway. This is a very difficult time for me. Twydi and I were friends since childhood."

"I can see that you are saddened about what happened to your friend," said Bitterridge, "and according to my generous nature, know that I will pay for any funeral costs. He was, after all, a very profitable Lesser and a good servant to the Noblatjs. Unfortunately, tragedy happens. We must face it and move on. The planned expansion of Heaven Sent into the larger global market is where you should be concentrating your energy now. This is what is important."

Rairai nodded. "Thank you, Lofty Bitterridge." He then turned and walked out the door. All the way down the hall he could not think of anything except the fact that he'd go crazy if he didn't find out exactly what happened to Twydi. He was desperate to know the truth, not just for the memory of his friend, but also for his own peace of mind. But what should his next move be? How do you find the truth in a world completely controlled by liars?

CHAPTER 26

There was a lot of noise downstairs…more than usual. Atira got up from the console and went down to see what was happening. As she stood on the stairs, she could see there were many strange Lessers standing in the hall. "I am sorry if we have disturbed you," said Taqwi who was also there. "These people have learned of this place and have come for sanctuary. I was trying to explain that there is no room for all of them. I wish there were, but where will we put them?"

Atira looked at the people before her. Their clothes were tattered, and they appeared tired and malnourished. The small ones looked thin and downtrodden. They didn't smile like children do. Her heart sank at the sight. Moloch feeds on such despair as this, and anything, no matter how small, that decreases his food supply is something to weaken the beast. "Do you know how to build?" she asked them.

An older man with white hair stepped forward. "I was…am a builder," he said.

"In the back, there is a maid's cottage. You will teach your people how to add rooms to expand it to make enough space for all of you. There is plenty of land to build new rooms. Can you do this?"

"If I have the materials, then yes. We can build rooms for ourselves."

Atira removed from her pocket the infolio she had taken from the saleswoman and threw it to Taqwi. "Use the funds from this to get the necessary materials," she told him. "Also, increase the amount of food and provide clothing for all of them."

Taqwi, who easily caught the infolio, smiled and replied, "Thank you. I will do this."

"Thank you, Mistress! Thank you from all of us!" exclaimed the builder.

"Do not call me Mistress," she said. "I am Atira."

CHAPTER 27

Rairai sat in the zippo-bar, scrolling through the contact list in Twydi's infolio. Most of those listed were casual business associates accrued since the launch of Heaven Sent. Not the type of people Twydi would have confided in.

There were a number of names marked with small red heart-shaped icons. Rairai knew these were Twydi's past romances, but he also knew it might have been years since he had last seen most of these women. Twydi had a habit of never being able to let go of their information even if it had ended badly. "Each one, in some strange way, is a part of me," he'd tell Rairai. "Deleting them from my infolio means deleting a part of myself."

Rairai took a sip of his zippo drink. He instantly felt the buzz. Just last week he had sworn off zippo, having heard it was not as healthy as advertised. Now, however he needed that little energized high to help keep himself sane. Despairingly, he stared back down at the infolio. Twydi, what happened? I need to know what happened to you. If only you could tell me.

He leaned back in his chair and stared out the window. There was no point in confronting Lofty Bitterridge. That would be suicide. And Twydi seemed to leave no clues behind. Rairai had gone over the apartment three times already, searching for anything that could help, but found nothing. Also, the police had no real interest in investigating. So, what was left? Where could he find someone or something that could point him in the right direction? Then, as he sat there slumped and despondent, he suddenly caught sight of something out of the corner of his eye...a familiar flash of color. Twydi?

Rairai sat straight up and leaned closer the window. It was not Twydi he was seeing, but a Lesser wearing a colorful jacket. Rairai could see from his crudely cut hair and his shabby pants and shoes that the man was a homeless Lesser who just happened to be wearing a very expensive jacket. Twydi's jacket! The same one-of-a-kind jacket Twydi had not been wearing when his body was found!

Rairai quickly jumped up from the table and ran outside. "Hey!" he shouted at the man who then took off in a run. Rairai ran after him. "Stop," he shouted. "The jacket! Where did you get that jacket?"

The man didn't stop but continued running even faster. Rairai was surprised that a homeless Lesser could run so fast.

The man was now so far ahead that Rairai thought for sure he had lost him but then suddenly, thanks to that brightly colored jacket, he caught sight of him again and watched as he turned up a walkway and disappeared into an opulent house. Rairai stopped. Why would a homeless Lesser have access to such a house?

As he approached the residence, Rairai began to wonder if there was something dangerous about this place. When he reached the walkway, he stopped and stared up at the second-floor balcony. The balcony door was made of the same one-way visionite glass as the windows so he couldn't see anything inside. He then cautiously walked up to the front door and paused to listen. It surprised him when he thought he heard the chatter and laughter of many children coming from inside. What kind of house is this? Regardless of how nervous he was feeling, Rairai knew he couldn't just walk away. He had to talk to that man and find out where he got that jacket. He reached out and rang the bell.

CHAPTER 28

A tira was used to hearing the hustle and bustle of the Lessers downstairs and had learned to find comfort in it. Their constant noise was an affirmation of life and reminded her of the importance of her mission. At first it was a little distracting, but now, she found that she worked faster and more efficiently with this chaotic background music. *Their beautiful clumsy song of existence*, she affectionately called it.

As she sat at her console, about to zero in on a new hotspot that had recently appeared, she suddenly heard strange sounds coming from the first floor. She turned from her work, towards the open doorway, and listened more closely. Atira recognized Taqwi's voice, but he didn't sound like his usual self. Often, she would hear him raising his voice to give instruction or to gently admonish someone who had violated a house rule, but she had never heard him fiercely argue before. She stepped out into the hallway to hear what was going on.

"Look, all I want to know is, where did that guy get the jacket? That's all. This is important!"

"This is a private home! You cannot push your way in here!"

Atira went to the stairs and walked half-way down. From here, she could see the people of the downstairs all crowded around and watching as Taqwi argued with a man standing near the door. She immediately knew that the man was not one of her people. His hair was too neat and his clothes too tailored. This man was a stranger and a wealthy Lesser.

"He says it's his jacket, not yours! I strongly suggest you go now!" shouted Taqwi.

The stranger, becoming more agitated, tried to push past him, but was immediately stopped by four strong young men. Atira let her fingers rest upon the quantum-eraser in her pocket and hoped she would not have to deal with this herself.

At that moment, Taqwi happened to glance up and saw Atira standing on the stairs. "Atira," he said, "this man is claiming that his jacket was stolen by one of ours, but Yukto says it is his."

Rairai turned and looked up at Atira. From her expensive dress, he assumed she must be the owner of the house. "I did not come here for trouble," he told her. "Only for the jacket. It's Twydi's jacket!"

Atira silently walked down the stairs, came up close to Rairai and looked into his eyes. For a moment, it paralyzed him. He didn't know what to say. Her presence left him feeling uneasy, yet at the same time, drawn to her. Quickly shaking off his confusion, he said, "Please understand, my name is Rairai Swyer. I followed a man to this house because I noticed him wearing my friend's jacket. I know it's his because it was specially designed. There is only one like it in the entire world."

"What man?" asked Atira.

"He's talking about Yukto," Taqwi explained. "Yukto is sometimes part of our group. He's been coming to the house for meals lately."

"Where is he now?" Atira asked.

"Yukto!" called Taqwi. Yukto shyly appeared, not wearing any jacket.

"Where is it?" shouted Rairai. "You were wearing it when you entered this house!"

"Obviously, you are mistaken," said Taqwi.

Rairai turned to Atira. "Please believe me," he pleaded. "This man was wearing my friend's jacket. I just need to know where he got it. You see, my friend was murdered. I need your help. Please! I have nowhere else to turn!"

Atira could feel his desperation and his pain. She knew he was being honest. "Come here, Yukto," she said. Yukto slowly, with head down, approached her. "I didn't murder anyone," he said softly.

"Where is this jacket?" she asked.

Yukto did not reply.

"Where is the jacket?" she asked again. "It does not belong to you and you must return it."

Yukto kept his eyes lowered as he answered, "It's behind the chair. The one in that room." He pointed to a doorway that opened onto the foyer.

One of the children, who had been listening with intrigue, darted into the room and reappeared holding a brightly coloured jacket. Happy to play such an important part in the adult drama, he ran up and handed it over with great ceremony to Atira.

Atira looked at the brightly colored jacket in her hand. She saw that such an expensive thing could not have possibly belonged to Yukto. She held it out to Rairai and asked, "Is this your friend's jacket."

"Yes," answered Rairai, taking it and examining it closer just to be certain. "Without a doubt, this is Twydi's jacket."

"And you say he was murdered?" Atira asked.

"I did not do it!" cried Yukto. "I only found him. He was dead already! He didn't need it anymore!"

Atira sighed, "You do not take things from the dead," she told him. "If you wish to eat at this house, you must follow the rules. Do you understand?"

"Yes," he sheepishly replied.

Atira then turned to Rairai and said, "If he helps you, will you keep quiet about this house and what you have seen here?"

Rairai looked at the crowd of odd Lessers in the hallway. What did he care if this strange woman was collecting these people in her house? He needed to find out what happened to Twydi. "I'll agree to anything you ask," he told her. "I just want to know what happened to my friend."

Atira looked at Yukto and said, "Now Yukto, it is your duty help this man. His friend has been murdered and you were the one who found the body. You must tell him everything you know."

Yukto was delighted he was no longer a suspected murderer. "Yes," he replied enthusiastically, "I will help!"

"That is good," said Atira. "We must help those in need." She then turned to Rairai and told him, "He will co-operate with you, and I fully expect that you will keep your promise."

"Thank you! Your secret is safe with me," exclaimed Rairai. "Thank you so much! This has been such a difficult time, and I didn't know where to turn. Yukto here, is my only clue at this point. I was just so lucky to have seen him when I did."

He then watched as the strange woman, without another word, turned and disappeared up the stairs. "Who is she?" he asked Taqwi, still feeling a little unnerved by her strange presence.

Taqwi smiled. "She is Atira. That's all you need to know."

CHAPTER 29

A tira watched from her window as Rairai left with Yukto. She was worried. Had she done the right thing by letting the stranger go? Was this one of the necessary times where she needed to use her quantum-eraser and she was missing an important opportunity? She knew the smallest miscalculation on her part could be disastrous to the mission. Her hand rested with uncertainty upon the weapon in her pocket as she watched the two men disappear down the street.

Turning back to the room, she stared at her console and the open panel that displayed her latest calculations. She knew for certain that all her numbers were correct. Numbers were reliable…never deceptive nor self-serving. Aliens, on the other hand, were another matter, and now a wealthy Lesser had seen something of what was going on in her house. Could she really trust that he wouldn't tell a Noblatj?

Atira thought about how she had been betrayed before on this planet…putting her faith in a wealthy Lesser who could not be trusted. Her loneliness had gotten the better of her, making her vulnerable to temptation. It was always a risk with any mission. This, however, was the first time she had slipped. Longing for her home, Atira, in her weakness, had merged with an unworthy mind and spoke to him of secrets. He then betrayed her to the Noblatjs. It would have been disastrous had they taken him seriously, but luck-ily the Noblatjs are believers in appearance only, and to them, she appeared very small and ordinary.

And even though she had trusted too much, she had not trusted with reckless abandon. She had not told him everything. It was mostly only hints at the truth. Still, many nights she wondered if she should have used her quantum-eraser instead of allowing him to live. Was she now making a similar mistake?

But then again, this was a much different case. There was no merging of minds to leave her vulnerable. There was no deep con-nection. There was only a single man who had been entrusted with a secret that was a very small part of the entire thing. Trusting, in this situation, seemed to be her best course of action. Also, this was a different sort of man, a different set of circumstances and she was now much more self aware of her own weaknesses.

Atira sighed. She hated that this whole thing had brought back those memories of *him*. Once more he was dominating her thoughts and threatening the mission. Walking over to the chair in the corner of the room, she eased her body into its instant molding surface. I must try to move my thoughts back towards the mission. My energy must be channelled in the right direction. She then began to focus on remembering the Queen of Dung. The Queen of Dung mission had been her first glorious success.

Reaching deep into the corners of her mind, Atira tapped into her internal memory-vision. In an instant, she was no longer in the room on the chair. She was now, once again, walking down that blood red carpet in that long narrow hallway, the reek of death as poignant as the day it happened. Her muscles grew tense and ready, and her flesh bristled in anticipation. She was the killer for the sake and sanctity of life.

The walls of the dimly lit hall were lined with pretentious por-traits of celebrated thieves and murderers. She walked past gener-ation after generation of Moloch's servants. Blood thirsty filth, all of them. Turning a corner, she then found herself standing before that dilating door. Her heart began to pound in a way she had never experienced before that day. Its strength and rhythm were filling her with a fierce and powerful force. She didn't realize until later, but this was her instinctual messaging system. It was a biological proclamation of justice echoing throughout the universe and a song of impending victory for her Naomh to enjoy.

Atira did not fear nor did she hesitate. Forcing open the door, she stepped inside and stared at the Queen of Dung who lay like a giant white maggot upon a divan fashioned from humanoid skin. The Queen of Dung was not what she called herself but was the name Atira had given her. Atira always felt it important to give names that were fitting and, given all the destruction the Queen of Dung had caused on that planet, this seemed more than appropriate.

In the past, when Atira used her memory-vision to take herself back to that moment, she wondered at the Queen of Dung's last thoughts. Did she know she was going to die? Could she feel anything besides blind arrogant disbelieve? Did she really have any idea who Atira truly was? Or perhaps there was nothing at all in her mind as she watched the strange alien rush towards her and plunge that stellar dagger firmly into her thick rubbery skull.

This time, Atira did not contemplate any of that. It was no longer important. She had moved well beyond this type of pointless speculation. It was now just a matter of doing what she had been sent there to do. Within seconds after plunging in the dagger, the Queen's eyes rolled up into her head and her doughy form rolled off the divan onto the floor. Atira then watched as she instantly dissolved into a pool of white goo upon those cold ancient stone tiles. It was a vulgar and messy way to kill her, but it was necessary. Her Naomh had explained that the Queen of Dung was so full of the power of Moloch that no other weapon would work except for a stellar dagger to the brain. *When the light penetrates the darkest part of the planet, the darkness will be dispelled,* he told her.

The wonderful thing about killing the Queen of Dung was not, of course, the act itself. There is no glory or satisfaction in the task of killing. No, the wonderful thing was the immediate aftereffects. It was for this reason that Atira replayed this memory. Within seconds of the Queen's death, the entire planet began changing for the better. It was an amazing and wonderful thing to feel…a warm rush of all that was good and beautiful in the universe coursing through her spirit and body. The first time Atira had felt this, she had come to fully understand the importance of her work. To feel such happiness replacing so much suffering and misery, made her know that all her sacrifices and hard work meant something. In her darkest moments in the missions that followed, she'd replay this memory to remind herself of what was waiting at the end of it all.

Now feeling calm and clear of negative thoughts, Atira closed off her memory-vision, let out a sigh and stared up at the ceiling. It was a fine animated sky-ceiling with billowing soft clouds…a special little touch she had put into the house when building it. She was glad the occupiers had not tried to change it the way they had changed some of the other rooms.

Atira's eyes now started to close. The soft vibrations from the chair had begun to lull her to sleep. Before her eyes closed completely, she happened to glance over at her console and was instantly reminded of all the work that still had to be done. She sat up straight. Moloch, although weakened, remained strong on the planet and there was no time to lose.

From downstairs came the sound of children laughing and running through the house. Atira smiled at their delightful noise and jumped up from the chair. She went over to the console and entered some equations…some she had used on the planet of the Queen of Dung. She then watched as graphs and maps suddenly appeared on the screen. Before she set to work, she took the time to remember her last words to the Queen of Dung. "You have wrought nothing but evil in this world. My Naomh has judged you fairly and handed down your sentence. Now, you are nothing more than a crumpled pig on the floor never to rise again." It was not bitter vengeful delight that made her say this. That would have been wrong and would have torn a new opening for Moloch to enter. Instead, it was a declaration of justice…a raw purifying declaration of justice… strictly for the delight of her Naomh.

CHAPTER 30

Rairai followed Yukto past the abandoned buildings to the edge of the river. This isolated area was where the Noblatjs had once built an experimental compound intended to program homeless Lessers into becoming a useful obedient slave class. The poorly conceived theories of their scientists, however, were quickly proven to be ineffective, and the project was abandoned along with the buildings. Now, there were only several severely dilapidated structures that once housed the laboratories and the cells.

Officially this entire area had come to be designated as The Badlands. The Noblatjs didn't want people remembering it for anything else. It was standard practice for them to rename things in attempt to try and deflect from their mistakes. The word Badlands made it seem as if the land itself was a fault, and not the Noblatjs who had failed so miserably at something in which they had invested so much time and money.

"This is where I saw them," said Yukto, standing in a spot where the sparse grass appeared to have been trampled down.

"And what exactly did you see again," asked Rairai who had already heard the story in the hovercraft but needed to hear it again to make certain Yukto was being accurate in his account.

"Like I told you, they dumped him here. Two big guys. They took him out of the hovercraft, carried him over and dumped him. I'm sorry, I took his jacket. I didn't think he'd need it anymore. I know it was wrong, but I had to. That's how I survive. I don't steal, but if I think someone doesn't need it, I'll take it. He didn't need it. I'm sorry."

"Don't worry about that," said Rairai. "Just tell me from which direction they came. I need to know their route."

"I saw them. I did. I saw them clearly," said Yukto, pleased at a further chance to redeem himself. "They took the west route in. I remember it well. They came from the west."

There was only one road through The Badlands, which ran parallel to the river, and Rairai had entered from the east. He was not sure what was down that western route, but if he could find a witness or surveillance camera, he may be able to learn more.

"Do you need a ride back?" he asked Yukto.

"No, I'm fine. My place is over there." He pointed to an abandoned building several yards away. "At least one of my places. I have stuff there," he said. "I collect things. Mostly stuff that comes down the river."

Rairai then took out his infolio and said, "Hold out your hand."

Yukto nervously held out his hand. Rairai placed the infolio over the man's palm and transferred a money print into his I.D. chip. "That is enough to buy a new warm jacket and more," he said.

Yukto, stared down at his hand, then up at Rairai. He smiled a huge smile. "Thank you! Thank you for this!"

"You're welcome," said Rairai, embarrassed by the fact that such a small amount to him meant so much to this man. "Take care and goodbye," he added awkwardly, then turned and headed back to his hovercraft.

CHAPTER 31

A tira anxiously paced back and forth in front of her console. She
had been visually accessing various meeting places of the Noblatjs, searching for signs of new alliances and schemes, when *he*
suddenly appeared on the screen.

There he was casually walking with a group of Noblatjs. She
watched as his head tilted in laughter at something said by one of
them. She used to love how he'd laugh like that. So free. So warm.
His laughter enveloped her...made her feel like she was somewhere
safe. But now, she understood his act. His smile and his laughter
were only parts of a performance, and she had just been another
prop in one of his personal productions.

It took her a while to learn just how deeply he believed in the
Noblatjs. He believed in their superiority and their natural ability
to rule the world. For a long time, he hid this from her because he
thought she was of use. From the beginning, he had sensed that
there was something special about her...something powerful. He
played along, hoping this power would somehow work to help raise
his status in the eyes of his masters. She understood that now. There
were perhaps even times when he told himself he cared about her,
but he was a liar even to himself. The only thing he ever cared about
was his servitude to the Noblatjs and what it could get him. It made

him feel important, almost like he was one of them. It disgusted her to learn it was all true, and it disgusted her whenever she remembered just how much she had shared with such a man. How she had made him a part of her.

To suddenly see him again was painful. She still felt foolish having believed he was different from the other wealthy Lessers...that he might be able to see beyond the limitations of his world...might be able to actually see her and be open to realities he had never imagined possible. But he was weak. He was just like the endless stream of mindless creatures she had met on countless planets. Creatures who professed to know about love, but who knew little to nothing about it. He's a dead end, she reminded herself. Just another pointless dead end.

Atira returned to her console. She understood she must get past this. The past was over, and she must now look to the future. She must stay focussed. There was work to be done.

Opening a new locator-map panel, she zoomed in on a large pulsing hotspot. It was clear that this was a Noblatjs' retreat. These retreats are where they go to receive their facial and bodily reconstructions or just to relax and socialize with each other. This particular one was a large elaborate complex nestled halfway up a mountain for maximum privacy and security.

Accessing the retreat's guest list, she now understood the reason the locator had identified this place. Thirteen of the names were part of a cabal she recognized. From previous surveillance, she knew about their objectives and why they would be meeting there. They were in the final phases of a global plan for the extermination of homeless Lessers.

Atira looked at the Noblatjs mulling about the grounds, splashing in the purification pool and being served by their loyal servants. They were so carefree, not giving a second thought to all the terrible things they had done in this world and were now planning to do. She wished there was even one who could be saved, but she had carefully scanned them all and found they were too infected with Moloch. There was no way she could undo their centuries of devolution. They were what they were.

Then suddenly, she caught a glimpse of shimmering fevor flowers growing in the garden near the pool, and she felt him creep into her mind once again. It was with a bouquet of these glowing blossoms that he had first welcomed her into his house. "I don't want to be without you," he said, as he offered them over like he was offering her the world.

O' the anguish of memory! A past that chains me and wears me down! Oh, lies! Oh, cruel lies! How could he? How could he have touched me and felt all that I am, and then, he chose them anyway? How is such heartless deceit possible? He laughed so warm and beautiful, and made my heart dance, yet turned from me to stand with the servants of Moloch. Was it all just fantasy on my part? Was he always turned away from me and I never noticed? Was there ever anything real about it at all? If not, then how did I come to be that blind…to lose myself in such an unkind illusion? To cast my treasure, to an opid-pig.

Anger was now rising inside of her. Burning its way up from her stomach, through her chest, up, up into her neck and straight to her brain. Before she left, her Naomh had told her, "There is just anger and there is unjust anger. You must learn the difference and release only the just anger. The unjust anger you must swallow and digest, but the just anger, you must release in the right places. When you release it, it will help to defeat Moloch."

Atira reflected on what she was feeling and decided it was right to feel this way. In the face of something as sacred as love, he had chosen Moloch. This was an affront to the universe itself. This was something worth being angry about and it was now time to release this burden out into the world. Reaching towards the screen, she gently touched the top of the mountain and then watched as it began to shake. There was a loud rumbling sound as the entire peak began to crack then fall away in pieces. A massive cloud of dust suddenly filled the screen and although she could not see it, she knew the retreat was now completely buried and all the Noblatjs who had been staying there were gone forever. Their murderous plans along with them.

"My anger has settled there," she said calmly, then closed the panel, knowing that it was best not to dwell upon it. Moloch thrives within temptation and it was a great temptation to enjoy power. Her Naomh had reminded her of that many times. Power is a necessity. That is all. Only a necessity borrowed from the universe. Never something to be coveted or desired. Once you do that, you are lost.

Suddenly, Atira became aware of a change, a shift in her senses. It was a lightening. Normally the planet weighed on her, heavy… dark and foreboding, but something had now shifted. It was still burdensome, but not as much. She took in a long deep breath and leaned back in her chair. Her choice had been validated. It was the right thing to do. Moloch was weakened.

It was true that she had dealt with anger on other missions, but this type of intense painful anger was different. It sprang from a place deeper than she had ever experienced before. The fact that she had managed to deal with it in a constructive way made her realize that her evolution was still ongoing. That was a relief. At times, she had worried that the damage might be too great, and it would spell the end of her. Evolution must continue if she were to reach the higher levels of being. That, after all, was another crucial objective to her mission.

CHAPTER 32

He was lucky. He knew that. There were not many of those older model surveillance cameras around anymore, but there it was on the road leading into The Badlands. Rairai had a collection of this old F-series equipment at home. Before Heaven Sent happened, he had spent countless hours taking apart his assorted pieces of obsolete technology and putting them back together again. This had been one of his favorite hobbies before the company took up all his free time.

He stared up at the camera high atop the pole. That thing should still be working. It's solid stuff, built to never break down. The only reason the F-series was replaced was because it was incompatible with the new red-flag system...an upgrade that allowed for the computer to better recognize suspicious activity and send an immediate warning to the Department of Watchers.

Rairai now pondered how he would get the thing down. Even when he was younger, he wouldn't have been able to climb something like that. Usually, there was a control panel somewhere to lower it. The new ones had special locking mechanisms, but this one would have been constructed when they were lock-free. He just hoped the panel still worked.

Kicking away the dirt and garbage at the base of the pole, he spotted what he was looking for. The small black control panel, once shiny, was now dull and scratched but otherwise seemed in good condition. Crouching down, he brushed more of the dirt away to find the release icon. "Now, just please work," he pleaded to the thing before he pushed down on it. He then waited, but nothing happened. Although the cameras were reliable, he knew the pole lowering technology had a reputation for being faulty. This was the reason no one had bothered to update this camera. But Rairai also knew there were ways around it. Likely, all that was needed was the right power boost. He looked around for anything that could work as an energy source, but all he could see was a complete pile of useless trash that had been illegally dumped.

Rairai then thought about his hovercraft. It ran on much newer technology, but it could work, theoretically. All he needed was to hook up the fusion generator to the panel and it should give it the jolt needed. The problem was that the energy from the fusion generator was so powerful it could fry the control panel, rendering the lowering mechanism permanently inoperable. He needed to do this very carefully.

After bringing the hovercraft closer, he opened the systems door and pulled out the fuelling wire. Positioning himself as far away as possible in case of an explosion, he crouched down then stretched out his arm and ever so lightly touched the fuelling wire to the panel. The instant they touched, there was a loud crack and a burst of light. Rairai was knocked violently backwards.

Stunned and lying on his back in the dirt and garbage, Rairai quickly gathered his wits about him. He got up then leaned in to examine the panel. "Damn it!" he cursed, seeing that his plan had completely fried the thing. How would he get the data-pin now? He sat back in the dirt, feeling frustrated and defeated.

Just as he was just about to leave in search of anything that might help, there was the sharp grading noise of metal grinding against metal. He looked up and saw that the pole was lowering. By overloading the panel, he had somehow managed to trigger the lowering mechanism. His plan had worked after all.

When the pole came to a stop, Rairai carefully removed the

data-pin. He stared at the tiny silver cylinder held tightly in his fingers. "I went to a lot of trouble to get you. You'd just better have something for me. Please have something for me!" He then quickly hopped into the hovercraft and headed home.

CHAPTER 33

A tira was certain all her anger had been dealt with. It had been worked out and now she could move on...concentrate solely on the mission. But what she didn't understand was just how deeply it had taken root. This was a new experience for her, and it was a surprise when, the next evening, her rage returned with a vengeance. *I cannot take this planet any longer! I cannot bear it! The madness of it all! The oppression and suffering! And* him*!* She picked up the glass sculpture and threw it as hard as she could. It smashed against the wall, shattering into a myriad of pieces.

She then stood silently and stared with satisfaction at the pieces of glass littering the floor. It had been one of the things left behind by those wealthy Lessers. It was one of their many gaudy trinkets that had filled the house. Most of the useless baubles downstairs were already gone. She had told the downstairs people to sell them for money. But up here, there were still too many reminders of mindless accumulation...symbols of all the meaninglessness Moloch had brought to this world.

These ugly disgusting things! Everywhere clutter! Representing nothingness! Why Naomh? Why do you want me to save this planet? Tonight, I want only to destroy it! All of it!

She looked over at her control panel and thought about how

easy it would be to put an end to everything in this world. Just a few quick data entries and KABOOM! it would all be gone. The Lessers, the Noblatjs and him too. All gone. She'd never have to think of any of them again. She'd be free.

As she stood there, staring at the panel and contemplating complete annihilation, sudden shrieks of laughter came bouncing into the room. Some of the children had run out into the grand vestibule and their sounds of unbridled joy were now echoing throughout the house. She listened as they clambered part way up the stairs then ran back down again. A sweet voice she recognized shouted up the stairs, "I love you, Atira!"

Meebelle's caring words made her smile, and the anger, that had previously threatened to consume everything, immediately dissipated. Now, it was replaced with a sense of remorse about the terrible thing she had just contemplated. How could she have gone there? How could she have been so weak?

Looking around the room at all the symbols of oppression, excess and waste, she reminded herself that, yes, it was horrible, but she had to be careful about falling prey to her own emotions. She had to remember her Naomh's warning. Never become so overwhelmed that you weaken yourself. To do that is to allow Moloch an opening. Anger is a power you must control, not something to be controlled by.

Atira then stared at the pieces of glass on the floor. She certainly did not feel guilty about destroying that thing. She knew that sometimes it's important to deal with rage by destroying something of no real value. If rage arises, and threatens to take immediate control, it needs to be focussed in a place where it does no harm. The shattered sculpture was a good thing…a release that kept her fury from moving to a higher level. She walked over and kicked the glass pieces into a neat little pile.

This entire room needs to be purified, she thought. All these foolish trinkets are things born from the emptiness of Moloch. So, why are they still here, cluttering the room? How can I properly concentrate surrounded by unclean things? Everything that has form accumulates a presence throughout its existence. The negative presence of these things…things coveted by those who once occupied my house and whose minds were rife with Moloch, are contributing to my problems. Tomorrow, I will have Taqwi remove it all and sell it. In that way, I will turn the negative into something positive...something the community can use. With it all gone, it should help me to control my anger. It's imperative that I master my emotions as I can't let anything, even what is inside myself, sabotage my mission.

CHAPTER 34

The image was a little grainy, but there was now no doubt in Rairai's mind. That hovercraft had Lofty Bitterridge's brand on the side. It was from his fleet and there was no logical reason for his people to be in The Badlands. The only possible explanation was that they were there to dump Twydi's body. At this point, all he could see in his mind was them carrying his lifeless friend and dumping him as if he were nothing more than a load of garbage. It made him sick to think about it.

What am I going to do? I can't go to the police. They protect the Noblatjs. I can't confront Lofty Bitterridge without serious risk to my own life. But I must do something. I must at least find out why. I'm so entangled with Heaven Sent, I couldn't walk away even if I wanted to. Especially with Twydi gone, Lofty Bitterridge needs me. I'm the story now. The narrative that Lessers can attain anything. All you have to do is believe and work hard to win the game. The Lessers who don't achieve are defective, lazy losers. I'm their ruse. The smokescreen that keeps the truth hidden…the truth that the Noblatjs are running a completely rigged game.

Although Rairai had had similar thoughts before, this was the first time it was crystal clear. Prior to this, part of him had always wanted to believe he was just as amazing and those infolio articles suggested. *"Lesser Success! Rairai Swyer Takes Company to a Whole New Level!"* It felt good, believing in the story. But now, in the face of Twydi's death, the truth loomed up like some giant long-fanged golo-serpent. It just couldn't be so easily denied any more. He was part of a giant hoax.

Rairai remembered back when they had first signed on with Lofty Bitterridge and how he was afraid that some sort of magic in Bitterridge's blood would see through the faked reports that supported Heaven Sent. Twydi knew the truth. Twydi knew this blood-thing was a myth. Sure, he was greedy and ready to play the game, but he never leaned on illusions. He understood how the world worked and he knew a lie when he heard it.

Rairai sighed at the thought that he would never be able to speak with his friend again. He had no idea that losing him would feel like this…like a part of himself was missing. He felt empty and alone. *What am I going to do now? I must do something…something to give meaning to Twydi's death. I can't let it end like this! I can't let Bitterridge just get away with it! But what am I going to do?*

He then remembered the strange woman in the large house and how she spoke to him with an air of authority. Was it possible she could help? What was her name? It was something he had never heard before. At…Atira! That was it! Atira. She had many peculiar Lessers in her home. Was she harboring poor Lessers, maybe even homeless ones? Who would do that in a world where everyone keeps in their place? Who would mix it up like that? Who would risk raising the ire of the Noblatjs by not conforming in such an obvious way? When she spoke to him, she had unnerved him. Made him feel like she knew something important…like she was capable of things. Could she help? The way she lives, she can't possibly believe in the Noblatjs. An ordinary person would be afraid they'd be found out…afraid of their 'all knowing' blood. But she wasn't like that. She wasn't ordinary and that's what he needed. *I must go speak with her…learn if I can trust her. I desperately need help and, right now, she seems like my only hope.*

CHAPTER 35

Taqwi opened the door and immediately recognized Rairai. "Yukto is no longer here," he told him and then began to slide the door shut.

"I'm not here to see him. I'm here to see the Mistress of the house," Rairai said, pulling the door open again.

"You're here to see Atira?" Taqwi asked suspiciously. "Why?" A few of the children had now curiously gathered behind him.

"Just, please...please tell her I am here. I don't want any trouble. I only want to speak with her."

Taqwi thought about it. He really wanted to push this man right back out the door...just get rid of him, but he knew doing this could cause complications. This wealthy Lesser had seen the house. He had seen the people in the house. He couldn't risk turning him away now. He'd have to call Atira. "Run and tell Atira someone is here to see her," he instructed one of the children. The child, happy to have such an important mission, rushed up the stairs.

Stepping back slightly, Taqwi allowed Rairai inside, then slid the door shut. Rairai now found himself standing with his back against the door and the much taller Taqwi staring down at him. He tried to think of something to say that would break the steely silence between them, but his mind was blank. So instead, he just stared silently past Taqwi's shoulder towards the staircase.

It didn't take long before Atira appeared on the stairs with the child behind her. When she saw Rairai had returned, she began to wonder if she had indeed made a mistake in letting him go.

"Mistress," he said, "I'm sorry to bother you, but I was hoping we could talk."

"What do you wish to talk about?" demanded Taqwi.

"That is a private matter," he replied.

"Anything you have to say, you can say in front of Taqwi," said Atira.

Taqwi gave him a slight grin.

"I just…" Before Rairai could finish he was interrupted by a loud banging on the door. Atira looked at Taqwi in alarm. Was this something to do with this wealthy Lesser? Had he brought trouble to the house? Had he deceived them after all?

But Rairai looked just as surprised as her and quickly moved over to allow Taqwi access to the door. Taqwi looked at Atira for instruction and she gestured to him to open the door. Taqwi then signalled to the children, who were still in the foyer, to hide. After they were all safely out of sight, he slid open the door.

Without warning, two police officers dressed in full protective gear pushed in and pinned Taqwi against the wall.

"What is this?" demanded Atira.

One officer, with weapon drawn, began to move further into the house. "You are suspected of harbouring homeless Lessers in a wealthy zone. This house is being confiscated and you are all under arrest."

Atira stared at the police. She knew there was no other way out of this. She discreetly took the quantum-eraser in her hand and, in the blink of an eye, the two officers were dissolved. Taqwi and Rairai were struck dumb by what they had just witnessed. Although they could not see the small quantum-eraser hidden in her hand, they knew Atira was somehow responsible.

"Taqwi, quick…lock the door!" she commanded, knowing she must work fast. Atira then ran up the stairs and, from her balcony, quickly dissolved the police hovercraft.

Next, she went to her console and hurriedly entered the necessary data. A panel popped up and, to her relief, she saw many weaknesses in the security walls of the Department of Records. With just a few quick taps, she was able to remove any trace of the two officers being assigned to her house along with any cross references to surveillance cameras. Before she erased the information entirely, however, she had a quick look at who had informed them. The complaint had come from the house directly across the street. She had noticed that couple peering out of their windows on occasion but hadn't thought anything of it. Now, she could see they were a threat.

Knowing she needed more than the quantum-eraser to solve this problem, she accessed the house co-ordinates from her panel. After entering in the destruct sequence, there was a thunderous noise and the room began to shake. She went to the balcony and watched as the house across the street was quickly swallowed by a giant sinkhole.

Atira stared at the cloud of dust rising from the massive crater and breathed in a sigh of relief. That could have been the end of the entire mission right there had she not done what she did, and the end of the mission would have spelled the end of this world and everyone in it.

She turned to go back inside, but then suddenly stopped when she saw Rairai standing in the doorway. For a moment, she wondered just how much he had seen, but then, from the look on his face, she knew he had seen more than enough. She placed her fingers upon the quantum-eraser.

CHAPTER 36

E veryone was on edge. Two Noblatjs had gone missing and there was no indication of where they might be. It was normal for Lessers to disappear, but Noblatjs? This was unheard of. Also, they were all still reeling from the tragedies of the dam burst and the avalanche. Four thousand and forty Noblatjs killed in all…instantly swept away by water and buried underneath rock and earth. How could such things happen?

Zylong stared out the window of the offices of Lofty Lyon. He couldn't help but wonder if *she* might have had something to do with all the mysterious things that had happened. He had always suspected she was from another world and could do things…powerful things. He knew she didn't like the Noblatjs. He also knew she was still somewhere out there. Sometimes, usually late at night, he felt as if he could actually sense her…walking, breathing, thinking, touching, smiling softly the way she used to. Don't go there, he thought to himself trying to shake off his intense memory of her.

"Zylong!"

Zylong hurried over to Lofty Lyon. "Yes, oh Greatness," he said with a bow.

"We have an assignment for you this evening. A particularly influential group of wealthy Lessers requires your charming presence at their party. We need you to sell them on the usual. Bring them on board with our latest projects. Be certain to remind them of all the good Noblatjs are doing, and also test their loyalty. If anyone says even the smallest thing that could indicate impertinence, I want to know about."

"Of course, Lofty Lyon" replied Zylong.

"I'm having the details sent to your infolio. Also, without being too obvious, see if you can find out anything about the missing Noblatjs. These Lessers may have heard a rumour or could possibly know something but are afraid to mention it. You can put them at ease. They'll tell you things that they wouldn't tell the police or one of us."

Zylong averted his eyes and said, "Yes Lofty Lyon, I will do you proud."

"As you always do," said Lyon, smiling at his favourite worker. He took great pride in the fact that Zylong's loyalty was unmatched. Among the Noblatjs, Lyon was greatly envied for owning such a prize. So many wealthy Lessers were now completely under his command because of this one man. Also, Zylong was proven to be very adept at swaying the opinions of other Noblatjs in his favour. Whether Lesser or Noblatj, Zylong was a natural at drawing them in and keeping them hooked.

"I appreciate your faith in me, Lofty Lyon," replied Zylong, all the while feeling guilty that he was not revealing his suspicions about her. It was true that, back when she was still with him, he had tried to talk with Lofty Lyon…to explain that she might be more than she appeared, but the Noblatj didn't believe him and he didn't persist. Should he have been more forceful then?

He desperately wanted to help them in anyway he could. This was extremely important to him. He took great pride in the way in which he served them, and how they doted on him for it. "So deep is your loyalty, that you are like a Noblatj," Lyon once said, making him feel like maybe he was as good as them. It was also true that they were the reason he enjoyed such a luxurious lifestyle. Without them, what would his life be like? He felt like he owed them everything.

At that moment, Zylong wished he could reveal everything he

suspected about Atira and the strange goings-on, but there was a problem. Telling could mean that his entire life would come apart. If Lofty Lyon finally believed him, he would certainly blame him for not warning him earlier even though he had tried. And if it turned out she were behind it all, he might be implicated and punished... possibly cast out or even framed for some unrelated crime. He could find himself living as a homeless Lesser, imprisoned or worse. All that he had built up over the years would be lost.

And although he wouldn't admit it to himself, there was the issue of speaking her name aloud and what it could do to him. He didn't want to say it. He didn't want to let it slide along his tongue once again, bringing back everything...all the sweet memories... the strange longing...the peace and tranquility...a sense of wholeness...a feeling of total freedom within that mysterious captivity. No, he couldn't allow it. All those things must remain locked safely within a secret dark room for which even he didn't have the key.

In the end, he decided it was best not to say anything. That was the safe thing to do and playing it safe was a way of life he had perfected. Just forget all about her and keep your mouth shut. Pretend she never even existed. Don't remember her. Just concentrate on your job and try...try not to think so much about anything.

CHAPTER 37

"The curious are coming," said Rairai, pointing past Atira and at the balcony door where, outside, he could see people beginning to gather around the sinkhole across the street. "It won't be long until the police arrive," he added.

Atira turned and looked out at the growing crowd across the street. She then heard the distant siren of a police hovercraft.

"They'll be asking questions...asking for identification. They could even be searching houses if they suspect something sinister," Rairai warned her.

She turned and looked at him. He was right. They would not just let this go. They would investigate. In the heat of the moment, she had reacted without taking this into consideration.

"I can help you," said Rairai. "I carry some weight as one of the owners of Heaven Sent. They'll listen to me. They'll believe me."

Atira wasn't sure. She didn't know what Heaven Sent was but did know that this man had come here wanting something from her. Could she trust him? What did he want and was what he wanted more than she was willing to pay? Just then there was the sound of the doorbell.

"The police are here," said Rairai. "And you can't just keep making them disappear and get away with it. You also can't just ignore them. They'll break the door down before they'll go away. Let me talk with them. I can handle it for you. I can help."

Atira did not reply, but instead pushed past him and headed for the stairs. Rairai followed after her. As she hurried down, she saw Taqwi standing in the foyer near the front door. He looked at her for instructions. "Go hide," she told him as she reached the bottom of the stairs. "And keep the others out of sight," she added, watching as Taqwi disappeared into the back of the house.

Atira then paused for a moment and just stared at the door, not sure what to do next. She knew the people on this planet naturally found her suspicious. She had a presence that seemed different... even unnerving to some. It was not always easy to hide among these aliens. Upon talking with her, the police would possibly want to delve deeper into her and this house. The doorbell buzzed again.

"You must let me help you," repeated Rairai who was now standing beside her. "You can trust me."

The police began to pound on the door, and she knew, if it was not opened soon, they would force their way in. She touched the quantum-eraser in her pocket, but then quickly took her hand away. Rairai was right. That was not an option this time. "Very well," she relented. "If you can help, then help us."

Rairai was relieved that she was finally willing to trust him. "Go up the stairs," he said, "and I'll take care of them."

Atira went up to the top landing where she would be out of sight but could hear what was being said. She listened as Rairai opened the door.

"Well, hello officers. How may I help you?"

"We are investigating the strange occurrence across the street. Show us your I.D.," said the tallest of the two men. He was obviously irritated that someone had not answered the door sooner.

Rairai happily offered over his palm which now contained his newly upgraded identification chip. The officer gruffly scanned it. On seeing the results, his scowl instantly changed to a broad smile. "Oh, Mr. Swyer!" he beamed. "I thought I recognized you. What an honor it is! My entire family uses Heaven Sent everyday. It's made an amazing difference in our lives."

"Hearing how much our magic little pill means to you and your family just makes me feel so privileged," said Rairai. "Thank you! So much! From the bottom of my heart!"

"Is this your home, sir?" asked the other officer.

"I'm just renting it short term. I'm thinking of buying it, but thought I'd try it out first. I was surprised to hear such a loud noise and then to see what happened across the street. The house was there and then, BANG, it seems to have just collapsed into the earth."

"Have you seen anything suspicious in the area? Anything or anyone who might have caused this to happen?" asked the tall one.

At the top of the stairs, Atira placed her fingers on her quantum-eraser.

"No," replied Rairai. "Nothing at all. It's all quite strange. Most likely a rare geological phenomenon. I've heard of it happening before. It's something to do with the weight on the surface of a pressure point versus the shifting plates of the planet. It doesn't occur often, but it when it does…well, as you can see."

"Hmmm…a pressure point. Makes sense," nodded the officer. Rairai was relieved that they seemed to be accepting him as some sort of expert in geological phenomena. It still amazed him how much he could get away with as a wealthy and well-known Lesser.

"Well thank you, Mr. Swyer," said the other officer. "We very much appreciate you giving us your time today."

Rairai clapped the officer on the shoulder. "It's just such an honor to know that Heaven Sent is being used by our heroes in uniform."

The officer smiled proudly and said, "We certainly don't want to take up too much of your time."

"Oh, it's been no problem at all," responded Rairai. "I'm so glad to have met both of you. You're doing a fine job…an excellent job!"

"Thank you again," said the officer as Rairai closed the door behind them. He then turned and saw Atira coming down the stairs.

"They're gone," he told her. "And I doubt they will be back. You see, I was able to help."

Atira walked up close to him and looked into his eyes. "You want something from me," she said.

Rairai couldn't help but feel a little nervous as she looked directly at him like that. After all, she had just made some people and an entire house disappear. "Uh, yes…that's right. I do require your help. Can we go upstairs and discuss it?"

Just then Taqwi returned to the foyer. "Is everything alright?" he asked Atira.

"Yes," she replied, "the police will likely not be back, but have everyone stay inside for today. We do not want to pique the interest of the curious who have gathered across the street."

"I agree," said Taqwi, surprised he didn't feel afraid after having just witnessed the frightening things Atira had done. Instead, it made him feel more assured than ever. To have a woman with that kind of power on your side was a good thing, and for the first time he realized just how deeply he trusted her.

"If you need me or if anyone else comes to the door, please let me know. I will be upstairs with…" Atira suddenly realized she couldn't remember the man's name.

"Rairai," Rairai reminded her.

Taqwi then watched as the man followed Atira up the stairs. He had many doubts about whether or not Rairai should be trusted. Before he was homeless, Taqwi had done business with enough wealthy Lessers to know just how deceitful they could be. They were mostly money grubbers with no ethics who would instantly turn on you in the blink of an eye. Now, there was one in the house. He didn't like it and knew he would have to keep a very close eye on this possibly dangerous man.

CHAPTER 38

Rairai stared over at the chair, hoping she would notice him looking and invite him to sit. It was awkward just standing there not knowing quite where to begin. Usually, in his business dealings, he would do a set up before the sell…charm them…put them at ease, but this was a different situation and she was definitely a different kind of person.

"My friend was murdered," he blurted out, surprising himself with this burst of forthrightness, "and I think…I think one of the Noblatjs had something to do with it."

Atira stared at him. Her expression didn't give him any hint as to what she might be thinking. Nervously, he shifted his weight from right to left and back again.

"I came here hoping you could help me. I don't know where else to go," he continued, feeling a little angry with himself that the words were not coming.

"There is no justice in this world," she replied. "There is no justice delivered when it comes to the Noblatjs. Did you not notice that?"

"Yes," said Rairai, "I know there is no justice. That is why I came to you. I sensed that you live outside of the unfair law. I saw what you did to those police officers. And I saw what you did to that house. I think that you are the only one who has the power to help me. I need to know what happened to my friend."

"Why is this important to you?" Atira asked him. "You are a man of influence and wealth. Are you not satisfied with that?"

"I should be, shouldn't I?" Rairai replied. "But I'm not. Twydi had his faults, but he was a good friend. He was also a good man who helped many people over the years despite his selfishness. I can't leave it the way it is. I have to know the truth."

Atira looked at him and wondered what to do. This was the first time anyone on any planet had ever made a direct plea for help of this sort. If she got involved, would it interfere with her more important work? The fact that he would pursue this at great risk to himself was admirable. Her Naomh had told her that she must encourage the best in people wherever she found it. If she didn't help him, maybe he'd give in and ignore the truth. His potential for evolution would be replaced by complacency. It was her duty to fight against complacency, promote truth and make the world a better place. This was important to defeating Moloch.

"Sit down and tell me all you know about what happened to your friend," she said.

Rairai broke out into a huge smile of relief. He wanted to hug her but thought better of it. "Thank you! Thank you!" he exclaimed. "I had nowhere else to go and no one to help. You don't know how much this means to me."

Atira didn't smile back. She had smiled back once before, and it got her into a lot of trouble. "You will tell me all you know about your friend's death and we shall go from there," she simply told him.

CHAPTER 39

Lofty Bitterridge stared at the information on his panel. It was a copy of Twydi's will sent to him by the Department of Death. It indicated that Twydi had left everything to Rairai. Bitterridge angrily closed the image with a wave of his hand.

I didn't imagine that you, such an idiot Lesser, would have thought that far ahead. If you had no will, everything would have gone to the company head…to me. It should have been mine. I suppose you were not as incompetent as you would have had people believe.

Bitterridge ran his fingers through his long blue hair and thought about what to do next. Should he simply let it go…wait for it to all go away? The suspicion Rairai showed about Twydi's death would likely fade quickly. Lessers did not have long attention spans and learning of the inheritance would certainly help him forget. Money makes Lessers forget a lot of things. Rairai would be no exception.

But as he thought more about it more, he found he couldn't let it go. Not this time. He had let go of too much over the years and it was time to change that. He was a Noblatj, and it was simply not right that Rairai should have all that wealth. It was becoming an increasing problem…Lessers not knowing their place. He and many of his friends could see this was true. They often discussed how the laws against Lesser ownership were not strong enough. Far too many of those lower brutes were making fortunes that should not belong to them. It was getting to the point where many Noblatjs were now struggling just to maintain their basic symbols of superiority. Lessers were sucking up valuable resources and threatening the rightful hierarchy of the world.

Bitterridge knew that the best thing for him would be to get rid of Rairai. It was his duty to his race and public decency. But before he could do that, he needed to ensure there was no will. That would take time. Also, acting too quickly and so soon after Twydi's death could raise suspicions. Although the police protected and worked for the Noblatjs, this did not allow for the overt eradication of wealthy Lessers. There were important appearances to keep up in order to prevent uprisings. The Lessers did, after all, greatly out-number the Noblatjs.

"Heaven Sent would not exist without me," Bitterridge reminded himself. "It belongs to me and only to me. I must take what is right-fully mine, and this Lesser must be eliminated. This is the way of the Noblatj, and our natural born right is to take whatever we want."

CHAPTER 40

"...and so, there is no one else to help me. That's why I came to you," Rairai said after having explained to Atira everything he knew about Twydi's murder. "The Noblatj's control everything, and there's not one of them who would care. A Lesser like Twydi is nothing to them." He sat tensely in the chair; his hands folded in front of him.

Atira, who was sitting in a chair opposite, thought about all Rairai had told her. She could see he was honestly upset about his friend's death and felt sympathy for him. At the same time, she had a huge mission to accomplish. There was a possibility that helping this man could interfere with the more important tasks at hand. She would have to carefully balance the risks.

"I don't know who you are," Rairai continued. "And I don't understand you at all. You seem to be something like a Noblatj, yet you are obviously very different from them. You're not a Lesser. But I don't want to pry or ask you a lot of questions about your identity. It's enough for me if you would help. I'm so desperate and I have nowhere else to turn. Please! Please help me!"

When he had spoken those words, 'I have nowhere else to turn.' She knew she would have to help him. *In your mission, pause to embrace all those who have nowhere else to turn.* That was part of the primary code set down by her Naomh.

"How do you feel about the Noblatjs?" she asked him.

"I think one of them killed Twydi," he answered. "What am I supposed to think of them?"

"How do you view their nature…their place on this planet?"

Rairai thought about it a moment and then said, "They…they are said to be connected… communicating through the blood. It's this superiority that gives them the right to rule over the world. They set the laws. They set everything."

"But how, in your heart, do you see them?" she asked again.

Rairai paused again, then answered, "I don't know if I've ever really honestly asked myself that question before. I've always taken the hierarchy for granted. It's just the way things are. But if I think about it, I don't like them. I know they say the Noblatjs are superior, but I don't think I feel it. Not anymore. I used to be afraid of them. Twydi even laughed at me for this. He understood more than I in this regard. But I don't think I'm afraid any longer. Something has changed. Something inside of me is different with Twydi gone. I'm not afraid now and I don't believe in their superiority. No…I don't believe anymore."

"Then, our goals are not that much different. I will help you and perhaps, when needed, and as you did with the police, you will help me."

Rairai sighed. It was such a relief for him to suddenly feel like he was now no longer alone in this nightmare. "Thank you!" he exclaimed, wanting to at least respectfully touch her hand in a show of gratitude, but holding back. Although she seemed to have a very warm and kind side, having helped the Lessers downstairs, she also seemed very guarded. He was not sure how his touch would be perceived and thought it best if he remained on the side of caution.

"We will begin tomorrow morning," she said. "Tonight, it is late, and I have other things to finish."

"Tomorrow, yes. I will be here tomorrow." Rairai got up from the chair. "Thank you again for your kindness." He then turned and quickly left the room not wanting to take up any more of her time. What he had asked for, he had received and was now feeling very grateful for that. He still wasn't sure who he was dealing with and wanted to tread very carefully with this strange woman.

As Atira watched him go, she suddenly found herself filling with doubt and suspicion again. This was not good. She shouldn't be feeling this way. Following her Naomh's code should be filling her with confidence and assurance. It always had before. This painful confusion was now overwhelming her. This was the damage caused by deception. A severed trust. Security ripped from her by an act of treason. Where was her solid ground now after being cast into the void of betrayal and lies? How was she ever to find her way back to trust again? "Just hold to justice and goodness and it will return," she reassured herself. "Keep to the true path and it will return."

CHAPTER 41

Taqwi stood in the open doorway. He was just about to knock on the frame when he heard Atira say, "Come in."

He stepped inside and saw her standing in front of her control panel with her back to him. She seemed to be concentrating on something. "I'm sorry if I'm disturbing your work," he said. "May I speak to you for a moment? Or if you are busy, I can come back later."

Atira turned and looked at Taqwi. She could feel that he was being sincere in his respect and regard for her work even if he didn't understand what it was, she was doing. It was a relief that he was not afraid of her after all that had happened and all he had seen. On her other missions, fear had often driven good aliens away which only intensified her loneliness. It was difficult enough being alone on this planet without losing even the possibility of friendship. "If there is a problem, you know you are free to come to me anytime," she said, warmly.

Taqwi blushed slightly. "It's just that…I wanted to say…about that wealthy Lesser. I've known his kind before and I'm not sure that you should trust him. Those types will say or do anything for profit, and they are almost always habitual liars."

Atira appreciated his genuine concern. "I'm not completely certain either," she replied. "But so far he has proved useful and he needs my help. He does not appear to worship the Noblatjs as many of the others do."

"But he does worship his wealth," said Taqwi. "That makes him weak and anyone associated with him would be vulnerable because of that weakness."

Atira smiled. Taqwi had taken such good care of the refugees and now he was proving to be so much more. He was contemplative. A contemplator with an equally strong sense of moral duty was not easy to find on any planet, but especially rare on this one. "You are right, and I assure you that I will be cautious. I will not let him interfere with my greater mission. And I will definitely not let him put you or any of the refugees in danger."

Taqwi instantly felt reassured. He trusted her. Even though he had seen her do things that seemed so harsh, he still trusted her. "Thank you for listening to me…for not dismissing my concerns as unimportant," he said.

"You're a good man, Taqwi," Atira replied. "You were caring for your people the day you showed up at my door. Selflessly, you have continued to care for all of those who have come here for sanctuary. Sometimes when I'm working so hard, and find myself wondering if it is all worthwhile, I hear the children playing or one of the refugees singing or I hear you giving instructions and organizing the day, and it reassures me about the importance of what I am doing. You provide me with hope and that is such a very precious gift. For that, I am so grateful to you." It surprised her that she had spontaneously opened up to him like this. Trust was beginning to return.

Taqwi blushed again. "I should go now," he said, turning to the door.

"If you have any other worries, you may bring them to me," Atira called after him.

"I will," he said before quickly leaving.

Outside the room, Taqwi paused for a moment in the hallway. Did she notice? He hoped not. If she did, it could complicate matters and that worried him. His first responsibility was to the community and he couldn't let personal feelings get in the way. Whatever he did, he must not let her see the desire in his eyes.

CHAPTER 42

Atira walked past three children begging in the shadow of the tower. Later, she would be sure to tell Taqwi to find out who they were and how they could be helped. At this moment, however, she had something very important that needed to be done and done immediately. It was not something that was a part of her original plan, but after waking that morning to the intense feeling of Moloch's oppression, she knew she had to do it. She needed to do it for herself…to help lighten the burden.

When she entered the building, she touched the small newly crafted device in her pocket. It instantly sent out a power surge that interrupted the surveillance equipment and caused all panels to crash. She then made her way quickly to the cyber-lift. "Top floor," she said as the doors closed behind her.

On her way up, she had a chance to think about it…remember back to what had happened. How she had been treated and how she had been ridiculed. Vengeance was normally not part of her mission, but Atira knew that she had to do something. This thing was not going away, and it was interfering with her work. She needed to lighten her mind. Righteous vengeance was sometimes an important part to defeating Moloch.

When the doors slid open, she came face to face with two large guards in full protective gear. "Do you wish to live or die?" she asked them.

They didn't answer, but instead made a move to lay their hands upon her. Atira did not hesitate to use her quantum-eraser. The guards were disintegrated.

Pushing open the opulent doors, she walked directly into the room and stood before the woman she had come to see.

Upon seeing Atira, the woman didn't seem bothered. Instead, she just remained calmly sprawled upon her bright fuchsia arro-bed. This large billowy piece of furniture was one of the many things exclusively available to the Noblatjs. The Lessers were allowed only to admire such things in pictures that appeared in the *Lifestyle* section of their infolios. These pictures were meant as a reminder of the importance of the Noblatj class and how they should always be revered.

"I've come to make things even," declared Atira.

Assuming Atira was a service Lesser there to work, the woman waved her arm in the air and said, "Then get on with it. There is quite a mess in solar bay. I had some friends over last night."

Atira did not move, but only silently stared at her.

The woman looked at Atira and for the first time noticed her fine dress. It seemed a little odd, but it was not that unusual for a service Lesser to be paid with a Noblatj's cast-off. She was just surprised such an expensive and beautiful garment would have been given to any Lesser. "Why are you just standing there?" the woman demanded. "You have a job to do, well get to work!"

"Do you remember me?" Atira asked.

"What? Why would I remember a Lesser?" The Noblatj was still feeling queasy from too much cya-drink the night before and was now becoming more agitated by what she believed to be an impertinent servant.

"It was at the party. Do you remember?"

"Party? What party? I attend parties nearly every day. Why would I remember a Lesser who served me a drink or food or whatever? And how dare you address me without proper reverence!"

Atira smiled ever so slightly and told her, "I've never served you. I do not serve the Noblatj."

Oh, that strange smile, thought the woman, where have I seen it before? Then suddenly, it came to her. "Yes! That weird one! I remember now. The one brought in by that pet of Lofty Lyon. What is his name? Zy...? Zylong! That's it! You were with Zylong. He seemed to think that you were interesting, but how funny you were? I remember that! Oh, the things you said. I don't know if I've ever laughed so hard. What are you doing here? Who hired you to work for me?"

"I told you," Atira replied, "I do not serve the Noblatjs."

The woman shook her head in disgust. Who did this Lesser think she was and how did she get into her house? "There is something seriously wrong with you!" she exclaimed angrily. "You really should be locked away. Where are my guards? How did you get by my guards?" She reached over to open the holographic panel that was built into the arro-bed, but it remained closed.

"There is no way out," Atira told her.

Hearing those words, made the Noblatj's bright vermillion hair bristle on the back of her neck. For a moment, she was stunned by this new experience. In her perfectly secure world, there had never been a need for her to fear anything. The pain and uncertainty that came with this new emotion was almost too much to bear, and she became intensely furious at being made to feel this way. Bolting straight up, she shouted, "Get out, you filthy Lesser! Get out! Get out of here! Help! Guard! Help!"

"You know nothing about me," said Atira calmly, "...or what I am capable of."

"You're a Lesser! I know that! And you will die for your insubordination! I don't care if you are mentally unstable! You will die!"

"No," replied Atira. "Today, you will die. But before you do, know that I am greater than you in every way. I am greater and I am stronger. And you...you are the one who is less." Atira then reached into her pocket and took out the quantum-eraser.

The Noblatj stared at the small unrecognizable object in her hand. "What is that?" she demanded, trying her best to keep her composure and not look afraid.

"This," said Atira, "is but a small insignificant thing in the world of the Noblatj...just like me...small and insignificant. It is also that which will put an end to you. I can see Moloch is strong within you, so I know this is for the good. What I do now, I do for the good of this planet and the universe." She then set the quantum-eraser on the slowest setting because if she was going to do this, she knew she had to do it right. It was how her Naomh taught her. For, in this type of a case, it was of no use if the person felt nothing. There was no balance in that, and balance was crucial. The person had to feel… to know that this was what they had wrought. Evil had to be made to acknowledge itself through its own pain. The suffering of Moloch could resound throughout the universe and serve as a warning. So, with a light tap of her finger, she activated the weapon.

The woman did not disintegrate instantly, as all the others had done. Instead, it started in her feet. Her feet began disappearing, until her empty red shoes slid from the end of the arro-bed and fell with a dull thud onto the floor.

The stunned silence of the woman as she watched her feet disappear before her eyes, quickly changed to horror as she saw her legs now begin to disintegrate. "What are you doing to me?!" she screeched. "Stop it! I command you to stop it!"

Bit by bit, the woman continued to disappear. She screamed louder and louder in the hope that someone…anyone might come to help. But no one did…there was no one to hear. It was the first time in her existence as a Noblatj that she had ever felt completely helpless. Prior to this moment, profound privilege was all she had ever known.

By the time her body had begun to dissolve, she went silent. Slumped back on her grand arro-bed, but very much aware, she watched as her hands vanished and then her arms. Her lower body was now completely gone, but she was still cognizant of what was happening. A slow quantum death severs the link between mind and body, so no matter what happened to her body, she would remain conscious to the very end.

Just before it reached her heart, a painful loss and significant point in the suffering of those who undergo this punishment, the Noblatj looked over at Atira. Without the strength to muster up any more outrage, she only stared with the empty stare of hopelessness.

This was the end…she had been beaten and beaten by a Lesser, and that would be her final humiliating thought.

Adhering to her training, Atira kept her mind free of all emotion as she silently watched the woman continue to fade away. She had to block out any personal feelings such as satisfaction, for satisfaction was a luxury and this was not about indulgence. It was about pure and simple equity. For it to work effectively, she had to keep it pure.

Finally, the bleached white face with its horrified bulging eyes made a strange gurgling sound then vanished. The bright vermillion hair was the last thing go. The Noblatj was dead.

This was the first time Atira had ever taken vengeance. Her Naomh had told her that vengeance was a balancing of energies only to be used very rarely and very carefully. She now hoped that she had been correct in her judgement and the situation did, in fact, make it necessary. If she had done the right thing, there should be an immediate effect. *For every balancing act against evil, there is a rippling of goodness throughout the universe.*

As Atira waited in the silence of the room for the sign, the seconds ticked by, and she began to worry she had made the wrong choice…let her emotions get the better of her. A wrong choice could have devastating consequences. Then suddenly, there is was! The relief! It came like a warm rain washing over her. She had broken through! Things were more balanced. The oppression was lifted. What she had done would now ensure she would be strong enough to complete her mission. That Noblatj, infected with the vacuity of Moloch, had left an imprint on her…an imprint that stood in the way of her work. In order to remove it, the Noblatj had to be removed and removed harshly.

Before leaving, Atira reset then opened the holographic panel in the arro-bed. She transferred all the money and real estate holdings into an intricate web of ghost accounts where they could never be traced. This would assist Taqwi and those downstairs. They would need it for their future. She then took one last satisfied look at the empty arro-bed before turning to go.

I am stronger and Moloch has been weakened even more. I have done a good thing today. I have chosen well.

CHAPTER 43

Taqwi was surprised when Rairai showed up at the door with a travel-carrier. "I need to see Atira," he said, pushing his way in.

"You need to wait here," said Taqwi firmly. He then disappeared up the stairs.

As Rairai waited in the vestibule, Meebelle and one of the other children peaked out from around the corner. "Hello," he said with a smile, which made them both giggle and run away.

"Come up," Taqwi called from the top of the stairs.

Not sure about leaving his travel-carrier, Rairai picked it up and headed upstairs. It was not too heavy. He had made certain not to pack too much just in case. As he followed Taqwi to the door, he had a sudden unsettled feeling. Was this a mistake? Would she misunderstand his intentions? What if it angered her? He had seen what she could do.

Following Taqwi through the door, he saw Atira sitting in a chair near the window. "Hello Atira, I'm so glad you could see me. I hope I'm not disturbing you," he said, trying to sound casually cheerful and not at all uneasy.

"She is very busy," interjected Taqwi

"I realize that," said Rairai, "but the authorities have been asking questions...to do with this house and that big hole across the street. It's getting serious."

"And what have you told them?" demanded Taqwi.

Rairai didn't want to talk to Atira through Taqwi. He could tell the man didn't like or trust him. "The same thing I told those officers the other day, that I am temporarily renting this house. It's why I'm here."

Taqwi then looked at the travel-carrier in his hand. "You want to stay here?" he exclaimed.

"For appearances, I think it's necessary," Rairai told him, setting down his travel-carrier which had now become a little heavy. "Temporarily, of course. It's just that they are very concerned about that hole, and there have been other things that are making them jittery. Noblatjs have died in accidents and some have even disappeared. They are all on edge and looking for any clues that could explain these happenings. Believe me, I've carefully thought about it and think it's the safest thing for you."

Atira eyed him suspiciously. It was one thing to help him with his problem, but to allow him to stay in her house? Would such a thing be a mistake she would regret? She simply couldn't afford to make any more mistakes. Besides, there was no room for Rairai downstairs, and she did not really want anyone upstairs with her. She found that being alone helped prevent distractions. Her mission had already been sidetracked once. She needed to keep focused.

"Please understand, I've thought very carefully about it and I don't see that we have any real alternative," Rairai told her. "You can't risk them taking a closer look into this house, and I need you. I need your help. Because of this, I need to keep you safe. Believe me, it's necessary for both of us."

Taqwi had been listening closely to what Rairai had to say. Despite his personal dislike for this wealthy Lesser, he was not one to allow his emotions to get in the way of the greater good. It was clear that Atira and the community needed to be protected, and this man could very well provide that protection. "I think he maybe right," he said to Atira. "If the authorities are asking questions, it is very dangerous for us. He's a wealthy Lesser and such people are known for their unwavering obedience. He would be considered above suspicion, and they would not investigate this house."

It was obvious to Atira how Taqwi felt about Rairai so, at first, she was surprised by his response. Then quickly, she understood and realized this was a very good thing. Not only could she trust him to be loyal to her, but she could also trust him to be loyal to the truth and the needs of the community. Such integrity was a very rare thing.

"There are two empty rooms on this floor," she said to Rairai. "You may have one of those."

It then suddenly occurred to Atira that this arrangement was not really fair to Taqwi who had shown such loyalty and compassion. If he were accidentally made to feel like he was unimportant, it would be detrimental to their relationship and to the mission. She had come to realize she needed him, and because of that, she must ensure his comfort and feelings of self-worth. "Take the other room for yourself," she told Taqwi.

Taqwi did not expect this. "Thank you, but I am fine downstairs among the others," he said, respectfully declining her offer.

Atira could see he would not easily accept such a privilege. He was devoted to the community and looked down upon any sort of luxury. She would have to convince him. "You do a lot for those who dwell downstairs. You organize. You provide. You decide. For this reason, you need a quiet place to think and relax if you are to continue being an effective leader. A single room is not much to take, and no one will say you don't deserve it. You work hard and you have earned a room of your own."

Before he had become a homeless Lesser, Taqwi had a nice place…a place of his own. Had he not insulted that Noblatj, he would likely still be there. But he had no regrets. He'd much rather be where he was, with a loving community, rather than alone pretending to be something he wasn't. After he became homeless, he fully committed himself to not taking anything other than what he needed and to be satisfied with that. Would accepting Atira's offer be breaking this commitment? He had to admit it was difficult trying to keep a level head downstairs with the constant chaos and noise. Everyday he had some new problem to deal with and no tranquil place to try and come up with a solution. Perhaps he should consider Atira's offer. Perhaps it wasn't about going backwards to a place he had happily left. Perhaps it was, instead, about moving forward to become a better more reflective leader. He also considered how she might have meant this as a gift, and it could be insulting for him to refuse. After this careful reconsideration, he told her, "Thank you. It could be a better thing for everyone if I were to move up here. I'll at least try it and see."

Rairai felt relieved that Taqwi would also be staying upstairs. The truth was, he was just a little afraid to be alone on the same floor as Atira.

Atira turned to Rairai and said firmly, "While staying here, you must know that I cannot have my work interrupted. You will not disturb me unless absolutely necessary. Do you understand?"

"Yes, of course," replied Rairai, who again picked up his travel-carrier from the floor. "I will absolutely not bother you unless there is a pressing matter to discuss. You have my word. Most of the day I will be in the office, anyway. I'll only be here in the evenings and I'll be quiet."

"Later, we will talk about Twydi," Atira promised him.

Taqwi gestured to Rairai that they should leave now.

"Then I'll see you later," Rairai said to Atira.

Atira did not reply, but instead got up, walked over and sat down at her console. She then began to enter data into the machine causing a number of panels to pop open. Taqwi again motioned for Rairai to follow him.

As they walked down the hall, Rairai thought about what a strange situation he now found himself in. There were so many unanswered questions. Should he have found out more about this woman before asking to move into her house? What exactly had he gotten himself into? He wished he could ask Twydi. Twydi was always good at dealing with uncertainties. He would have known how to handle himself in midst of the unpredictable.

As they stopped in front of a closed door, Rairai turned to Taqwi and asked, "I don't mean to pry, but do you know what it is Atira is doing? What kind of work is it, and why is it so important?"

Taqwi looked at Rairai and laughed. "Haven't you figured it out by now," he answered. "She is here to save the world, of course." He then touched the button on the wall and the door slid open.

Rairai laughed even though he wasn't entirely sure if Taqwi was joking. He then stepped inside the room and the door slid shut behind him.

CHAPTER 44

Atira sat at her console and carefully studied the map in front of her. From their previous patterns, she could see exactly where they were planning to go next. Over the years, the Noblatjs had been pushing Lessers off their land and forcing them to live in small nomadic groups. If she were to block their next planned appropriation, it would slow them down and weaken their resolve. This was only one part of the bigger picture, but an important part. The weaker and more unstable they were, the better.

The Noblatjs had been so careful and strategic in their takeovers, that the Lessers didn't really know what was happening until it was finished. By then it was too late to try to do anything about it. Also, the Noblatjs controlled all the information and news transmitted to the infolios, so it was easy for them to keep these takeovers hidden from the larger Lesser population. This suppression of the truth and promotion of ignorance would have to change, but first Atira needed to deal with the urgent matter at hand.

She touched the point on the map where she had decided her defensive would begin. It was a spot on the edge of a canyon. Then tracing a slow winding line with her finger, she came to a stop at the base of a protective mountain range. After entering the code, she quickly brought up another panel and punched in the co-ordinates to provide her with a live aerial view of the area.

The view showed a fleet of armed industrial hovercraft moving in the direction of the Lesser communities. From information she had previously gathered, she knew the Noblatjs weren't planning to simply drive the people out this time. This time they planned to drop fazzo-gas...a new weapon they developed that would instantly freeze flesh, killing all life within a three hundred iben radius. They had to be stopped!

Waiting until the fleet had reached the defence line, she then initiated the sonic plate-shifter and watched as the ground underneath began to tremble. Within seconds, a large jagged crack ripped thunderously through the earth, opening wider and wider and causing the heavy hovercrafts above to wobble and shake like toys. As the pilots fought to regain control of their ships, a huge wall of water suddenly gushed upward from the crevice, instantly enveloping the entire fleet. Then as quickly as it had risen, the water fell back down into the gash. Everything was now still and, where she had drawn the defence line, was now a valley with a beautiful turquoise fresh river running through it. There was no sign of any hovercraft.

Atira leaned back in her chair and breathed in a sigh of relief. She knew this loss would frighten the Noblatjs into believing the area was too geologically unstable to be profitable. They would not trouble these Lessers again, and their plans to live-test the fazzo-gas would have to be put on hold. It was only a small step in saving the entire planet, but it was a crucial one. Had this been a success, it would have led to a quick succession of land grabs and more mass-murder.

As she now admired the beautiful valley and winding river she had just created, she felt her heart suddenly leap with joy. *Oh, joy!* On her planet joy was a continuous state of being. There was only joy. In this world, she was made to wait for moments like these... those times when she would actually see and feel goodness manifesting. What treasures these were...those moments where all the darkness of doubt was chased from her mind and she could feel the glorious reassurance that all her hard work was not in vain. But this joy was not hers alone. Like all such joy, it resounded throughout the Universe as a shared experience of the Life-Law: *For every act of righteousness and justice, something beautiful is born.* And now, here was this magnificent river birthed from an act of justice, and in its beauty, it would create a fertile valley and provide a much needed source of water for the Lessers who lived nearby.

"Atira," a voice softly called from behind her.

She turned and saw Taqwi in the doorway. "Come in, Taqwi," she said, feeling happy to see him. His presence was only adding to her good mood.

"I hope I'm not bothering you. If this is a bad time, I can come back."

"You are no bother," she said, "and I have just finished my work for the moment." Taqwi had surprised her in so many ways. His respect and his understanding were things she had not been expecting to find. After Zylong…after that mess, she had lost so much of her trust and hope. The intelligent and honest understanding Taqwi had of his world's situation along with his devotion to the community was proving to be a great source of comfort for her. He had accomplished a very difficult task by providing a sanctuary of goodness in a very cruel world, and she felt so lucky to have found someone whose strength and resolve was inspiring her to trust and hope again.

"It's just that we have a problem," he said. "We are out of funds, and the people will be needing more food." He then handed over the infolio she had taken from the saleswoman. "As you can see, the account is now empty. You've done so much for us and I hate to ask more of you, but our supplies are low and in a couple of days there will be nothing left to feed the community."

"That is no problem," said Atira, taking the infolio and turning to the console. She took one more look at the large beautiful river she had created before switching the panel over to the main banking system. By instantly taking small amounts from Noblatj accounts from all over the planet she was able to load up the infolio with enough funds for several years. "Here," she said handing it back to Taqwi.

Taqwi looked down at the amount and couldn't help laughing.

"Why do you laugh?" she asked.

"It's just…how they view money…how you just hand it over like it is nothing. This is so much money."

"It is nothing," said Atira. "Money is all a child's fiction. Something to keep the Noblatjs feeling like they are important and to keep the Lessers down."

"Yes…I suppose it is," replied Taqwi. "I never thought of it that way…it is a type of fiction.

"To understand money, you must see it as it truly is. Nothing. It is nothing at all. But it's a nothing this world was built upon, so we need it for survival. We do not worship it or covet it. It is a nothing we deal with. We can never allow ourselves to be consumed by its vacuous nothingness. If we do, then we are lost…as lost as any Noblatj."

Taqwi nodded as he wondered what a world would be like where money was not valued above life. He had certainly seen how much pain and suffering it had caused. Was that the kind of world Atira was working to create? As he looked at her face, he felt a strange stirring of emotion. She had made him think about so much and re-examine so many things. In that moment, he just wanted to know more about her…draw her out. "That day," he said. "The day we came to your door. We almost walked by. The little ones were so tired, and we had been turned away by so many. We almost just gave up and left. I was getting worried about being arrested and what that would do to the children. I'm not sure why, but I looked at your door and thought, 'one more try…just one more try'. And now, here we are. Sometimes I think, what if I didn't? What if I had given up and we had just walked on by?"

Atira got up from her chair and stood face to face with him. "Sometimes our hearts guide us to important places where our reason cannot go," she said, noting the strength in his gentle eyes. "That is why we have hearts. It is our hearts that save us, even if sometimes it seems our hearts will be the end of us." She surprised even herself with this impromptu speech, having cursed her own heart so many times recently.

Taqwi felt suddenly flushed at her words. Embarrassed and worried she might notice, he turned away saying, "I should go now…

load up on supplies. Some of those children eat more than many of the adults." He then quickly left the room.

Atira stared after him. The connection between them was growing, but she knew she had to be careful. Her heart could be a helpful source of great power, but when headed in the wrong direction, it could also slow down her work as it did once before, and nothing was more important than the mission. She knew she had to maintain her focus. Time was running out.

CHAPTER 45

Rairai had unpacked the few things he had brought with him and was now carefully examining his new abode. It was a large room with tall windows that looked out into the back garden. There was nothing much in the way of furnishings besides the built-in bed, a cupboard, a chair and a small table. The marks on the floor seemed to indicate that the room had recently been filled with furniture. There were also many small holes in the wall suggesting that many hanging objects had been removed. Ostentatious decorating would have definitely been the norm in a house like this and Rairai wondered where everything had gone.

The air in the room was stale, so he walked over and slid open the window. A fresh breeze blew in, carrying with it the happy sounds of children. He looked down into the garden and could see about twenty children running about and playing. It surprised him to know just how many were living here… homeless Lessers, all of them. How many times had he passed such children on the street… looking so discouraged…begging for anything he could spare? Yet here were these same children so well-fed, so well-dressed and happy. Whoever this Atira was, she was certainly being kind to them.

Suddenly, one of the children shouted out a name that sounded a lot like Twydi and the image of Twydi's battered body lying on that cold steel table flashed before his eyes. Sadly, he leaned his head against the window frame. I know it's madness, he thought, and I know I'm risking everything, but I just can't let him go like that. He was mercilessly murdered then discarded like some worthless piece of garbage. He was my friend…my best friend.

Rairai then thought about Atira and her promise to help. He believed she could do it, but also knew she would first need access to Lofty Bitterridge. She needed to be on the inside, so she could fully understand what he was up against. It wasn't enough just to have her zap him from afar with that thing. That would not only complicate things with Heaven Sent, but it would also not give him the truth, and he needed the truth to move on. For Twydi's sake and his own, he needed to know everything!

Suddenly, there was a knock on his door. Before he could answer, it slid open and Taqwi stuck his head inside the room. "We will be eating soon," he said, "if you want to join us."

Rairai hadn't thought about food or where he'd eat while living in this house, but suddenly he did realize he was very hungry. Was it right to eat with those downstairs? He didn't want to take their food, but neither did he want them to think he considered himself above joining them. Quickly deciding that it was important to put in an effort, and that he could always make a financial contribution later on, he answered, "Thanks, I'll be down soon."

As Taqwi turned to go, Rairai asked, "Taqwi, will Atira be eating with us?"

Taqwi stopped and turned to look at him. "Atira does not eat with us. She eats alone. I bring the meals to her."

"Oh, I see."

"Her work is very important. She doesn't have time for much more."

"Maybe it's time to change that," suggested Rairai. "Everyone needs some social interaction."

"She's not everyone. She's unique," said Taqwi defensively.

Rairai found himself suddenly wondering about the relationship between Taqwi and Atira. Were they more than just associates with a common goal? Were they perhaps friends? Were they even lovers?

ALIEN ATIRA

If they were, he wasn't sure what to think about that. At this point, he wasn't sure what to think about anything. Nothing really made much sense anymore. Or maybe it made more sense than ever. He couldn't really decide which it was.

"Where did she come from?" asked Rairai. "She's not from this planet, is she?"

"I never asked her," replied Taqwi. "For some reason, it never seemed important. It only seemed important that she is here."

CHAPTER 46

"I need a date," said Rairai. "It's one of the most important No-blatjs' parties of the year and I need a date. Will you attend with me?"

Atira didn't answer him. The thought of finding herself among the Noblatjs and the elite Lessers again was unsettling. It could also be risky. Zylong would be there. Why wouldn't he be? A high-pro-file party like that. She couldn't be certain just how much he had told them but suspected that it was most of what he knew. She was just relieved she had not been more open with him. Even with the few things she had revealed to him, she knew he would not be able to put much of it together. He was far too self-absorbed to be that perceptive.

"Lofty Bitterridge will be there. I can introduce you," Rairai explained as he began to worry that maybe she had changed her mind about helping him. "If we are going to come up with a plan to uncover what happened to Twydi, you will need to get inside the world of the Noblatjs."

"Some of them may know me already," Atira confessed.

"You have been in contact with the Noblatjs?" Rairai was surprised.

"I…" Atira didn't like having to explain herself to aliens. She had learned that they did not easily understand and were often quick to judgment. "I had previous contact with them through a wealthy Lesser."

"A wealthy Lesser?"

"His name is Zylong."

"Zylong! Everyone knows who Zylong is. He's a hero for wealthy Lessers everywhere. They aspire to create the kind of alliances with the Noblatjs that he has managed to make over the years. Twydi absolutely idolized him."

Atira did not want to talk about Zylong at all, but she had already agreed to help Rairai, so it had to be done. He had to know, and her Naomh had told her that she must never go back on her word out of fear or discomfort. Only if it was for the greater good could she break a promise, and unfortunately, this was not one of those times.

"How did you meet him?" Rairai asked.

"It was an accident," she explained. "I happened to be outside of the Ministry of Communication assessing its power and capabilities. He came up to me. Spoke to me. I had to pretend I was someone else. A woman lost."

"He's charming. I've seen him in action once. The way he wraps those Noblatjs around his little finger. It's fascinating. Did he charm you?"

Atira wanted to explain how lonely it was on a strange planet. How isolated she was as the only one of her kind. Make him understand how that isolation can sometimes eat away at you. How there are times when you are so desperate to feel connected to something...anything, that it leaves you weak and vulnerable to foolish choices. Instead she simply answered, "I suppose he did."

"How long were you...in his company?"

"Too long," she replied. "But I did wake up to see this was not a good place to be. I did walk away."

"So, if you went to this party, there would be Noblatjs there who know you?"

Atira sighed. "Some may know something of me. I had attended a few parties with Zylong but talked very little. They likely know only what Zylong would have told them. Most of them have probably forgotten all about me by now. They only ever saw me as a hang-er-on Lesser."

"What exactly does Zylong know?" Rairai said, thinking of how little he himself knew.

"He doesn't know about this house, my quantum-eraser or the console. He knows I am… different…capable of things, but he's not certain of what. It is, however, possible that an air of suspicion could follow me into this party. You must know that beforehand, if I am to accompany you."

Rairai thought about it. It could be risky taking Atira but search-ing for the truth was risky no matter what. On the other hand, it might be to his advantage if Atira was familiar to them. They wouldn't think he was bringing a complete stranger into their midst. It could make them less likely to pry and look more deeply into her background. He also had to admit that there would be a sense of pride walking in with a woman who had walked away from the great Zylong. That could make for a very interesting evening.

"The way I see it," he said, "they would be suspicious of you no matter who you are. They're suspicious of all Lessers, but especially of those who are strangers to them. At least they have seen you before. That could put them all at ease. They are so egotistical and so sure of their positions that it's doubtful they would see you as some sort of threat."

"Or seeing me again could make them mistrustful towards you," she added, knowing that she was not being honest. They could possibly be a little suspicious of her, but they wouldn't assume that much about Rairai. She simply did not want to go…didn't want to face Zylong again. Such an encounter worried her on several differ-ent levels.

Rairai smiled. "Somehow, I don't think we have to worry about that. Of course, we'll be careful, but you always must be careful around the Noblatjs. That's just common sense. Anyway, we should prepare ourselves a story to tell them in case they ask any questions about us…about our relationship."

"Of course," Atira replied, relieved he didn't ask any more ques-tions about Zylong. She then began contemplating the party in relation to Universal Law. Her Naomh had once told her, *remember that there is nothing simple about the Laws of the Universe. The intricate ways in which they work is unfathomable. You need only know that 'surprise' is a force that can help bind the good energies. Stay true to your mission and whatever surprises may come your way will work for you, not against you.*

Atira understood this to mean that if something unexpected and potentially unpleasant suddenly comes her way, she must not assume it will be detrimental. She must embrace what is offered even if she is unsure about it. The Laws of the Universe are on her side just as long as she stays true to her mission and to her Naomh. With this in mind, she turned to Rairai and asked, "So when exactly is this party? I will need a new dress."

CHAPTER 47

"You did a fine job with Lofty Tannerpug," Lofty Lyon said, his mouth close to Zylong's ear. "She will be an asset to my upcoming project."

"It was a team effort," replied Zylong, trying to sound as humble as possible while feeling just the opposite. He was very proud of the way he had convinced that Noblatj to join up. Many others wanted her support, but only he was able to procure it.

Lofty Lyon laughed. "No, my friend, it was you who did it. You have the gift of persuasion. A natural gift."

Zylong beamed at being called a "friend". Was Lofty Lyon finally beginning to see him as an equal…a Lesser as worthy as any Noblatj? He hoped so. He had worked hard to gain his respect. "We still need to get all the money," Zylong said. "I haven't yet convinced her to fully invest."

"I am certain you will have no problem with that," laughed Lofty Lyon. "When she arrives, be sure to provide her with all the attention she will be wanting. Remember though to hold back. Tease her a little, the way I taught you to do. You'll do well if you remember all you have learned from me."

Zylong found himself getting annoyed at Lofty Lyon's comment… annoyed that the Noblatj should take credit for his own innate business prowess. Quickly though, he reminded himself that he, as a Lesser, had no right thinking such things. The Noblatjs were of the pure blood and he was tainted. He knew better than to let such thoughts manifest. "I will try my best to serve you well," he simply replied.

The two men were standing on a raised floor that led outside to the garden area. From there, they could look out over the party room and know exactly who had arrived. The place was now quite full, mostly with Noblatjs. Scattered throughout the crowd were several Lesser elites, easily recognizable by their facial alterations, clothing and hair styles. Being forbidden from adopting any of the fashion styles of the Noblatjs, but wanting to distinguish themselves from ordinary Lessers, they had developed a style all their own, not quite as garish as the Noblatjs, but very close.

"Oh, just look at Lofty Bitterridge over there!" said Lofty Lyon. "He's so full of himself since discovering that little magic pill. Magic! It's full of nothing! He sells them nothing! Empty, empty little dreams. That can't last. Just wait until my new project is unveiled. He will choke on his envy."

Zylong felt nervous and uncomfortable whenever Lofty Lyon spoke that way about another Noblatj. He liked to imagine that all Noblatjs were perfect. It gave him a sense of security and order. To hear any one of them spoken about with such disrespect left him feeling vulnerable and unsure. But what could he say to Lofty Lyon without sounding disrespectful? Nothing. So, he remained silent.

"And look at who is with him. It's his little magic pill Lesser," said Lofty Lyon. "The one who is still alive at least. What do you think happened to the other one, Zylong? Hmmm?"

Now Zylong was feeling even more uncomfortable. "I…I heard he mixed with the wrong people," he said.

Lofty Lyon laughed a big hearty laugh and then slapped him on the back. "That's right, Zylong. Never mix with the wrong people. Something every Lesser should remember." It was then that Lyon noticed someone standing next to Rairai. "…and who's that woman with him?", he asked. "She looks familiar." Then once again Lofty Lyon burst out into laughter. "Why Zylong, isn't that someone you know? Isn't that the one who was once with you?"

Zylong looked over to where Bitterridge was standing and was completely caught off guard to see her again. She was dressed in a shimmering full-length gold colored gown that, although not as elaborate as the Noblatjs fashion, made her stand out against all the other women in the room...Noblatjs and Lessers alike.

"Why yes, it is her!" exclaimed Lofty Lyon. "The one you once tried to convince me was magic. And look! It turns out she's very magical. She has magically replaced you with that little pet of Lofty Bitterridge." He laughed aloud again.

Zylong could feel the heat rising to his face. He wanted to reply to Lofty Lyon with some witty quip. He wanted to laugh about it too. But he couldn't. All he could think was how good she still looked and how much he wanted to talk to her again.

CHAPTER 48

S he could sense him. He was close. This was one of the stub-
born side effects of having mind-merged with him. That act of
intense intimacy had left a connection that was beyond space and
time. It's why his memory haunted her every day and why every day
she worked to permanently sever this strand of connected thought.
There were days when Atira wondered if she'd have to live with this
burden for the rest of her life. *Why did I ever allow this to happen
with such an alien? Why did my Naomh not warn me about it before I left for this planet? I was warned about many things, but not
this. I didn't know this would happen.*

Atira tried to push the thought of him out of her mind by turning
her attention back to the conversation between Lofty Bitterridge
and Rairai.

"Perhaps you would like to join me sometime at my house on the
lake. Both of you, of course," said Lofty Bitterridge, grinning a neon
blue grin. His bleached white hair was interlaced with red ribbons
and piled elaborately upon his head. "We could go fishing, Rairai.
Out on my boat. The lake is very deep with plenty of fish."

"That sounds wonderful, doesn't it?" Rairai said, gently nudging
Atira who he sensed was not paying attention.

"Oh…yes…" Atira replied, "it sounds wonderful."

Before she could say anything else, a familiar voice interrupted. "Lofty Bitterridge! What a great honour it is to see you here tonight!" They all turned to see Zylong walking boldly up to the group.

Atira felt her entire body tense up. All she wanted was to get away as quickly as possible...to run out of that room and out of that party, but she couldn't do it, not without it looking obvious. She needed to remain where she stood and summon up her deeper strength.

"Zylong!" said Bitterridge. "Where is Lofty Lyon and why has he let you off your leash?" He laughed a hearty laugh.

"Lofty Lyon is just over there, if you'd like to speak with him," said Zylong, hoping Bitterridge would leave and Rairai with him. He wanted to speak to Atira alone.

"Not just now," replied Bitterridge. "Have you met the genius who has given us Heaven Sent? This is Rairai Swyer."

Zylong smiled at Rairai. "No, we've never met before. How do you do, Mr. Swyer?"

"Please call me Rairai, and it is a pleasure to meet you. I've been wanting to meet you for some time now."

"And this," said Bitterridge, "is his charming companion, Atira." Bitterridge had actually seen Atira with Zylong before but didn't recognize her as all Lessers looked mostly the same to him.

"I believe we know each other already," said Zylong.

"We have been previously acquainted," said Atira without smiling, and glancing at him only briefly.

Bitterridge could see the tension between them and grinned at the Lesser drama. "And how do you know each other?" he asked, hoping to stir up more trouble.

However, before anyone could respond, Lofty Lyon suddenly appeared, clapped Bitterridge on the back and loudly declared, "So how's business, my friend?"

"Oh, it is brilliant! Absolutely brilliant! And this here is my lucky charm, Rairai Swyer, of whom you have heard so much. And this, of course, is his lovely companion Atira."

"Yes," said Lyon, smirking. "I've met Atira before," he added, glancing with amusement over at Zylong.

Bitterridge chuckled a little to himself at the awkward situation, but before he could say anything to make it even worse, Rairai interjected, "What an honour this is. To find myself in the presence of two of the greatest Noblatjs to ever live. Surely, I am the luckiest Lesser on the planet."

"Ha!" said Lyon. "You must indeed feel like you are in a dream to rise to such a level as this."

"A dream, yes!" exclaimed Rairai. "A wonderful dream!"

Out of the corner of her eye, Atira could see that Zylong was trying to move closer, and she worried about how she was going to manage to move away discreetly. Feeling his presence was bad enough. She couldn't let him get any closer and certainly had to protect against him touching her even briefly. Such things would only intensify the residual effects of the mind-merge and weaken her. She had to keep up her defences.

Just then and to her relief, Lyon said, "I see Lofty Tannerpug has arrived. Zylong, go greet her and make her feel comfortable."

Zylong looked over at the entrance and could see Lofty Tannerpug chatting to another Noblatj while her eyes busily scanned the room. He knew she was looking for him. "As you wish, Lofty Lyon," he said, trying not to let his annoyance show. He desperately wanted to speak with Atira. She had left so suddenly and unexpectedly, and there was still so much he wanted to say. He also could not forget the beautiful feeling of being inside of her mind. "Please, excuse me," he said to the group, as he tried to discreetly catch Atira's eye. She, however, looked the other way.

After he was gone, Atira felt like she could breathe again. It was a relief knowing he'd now be far too busy to come close to her again this evening. Although feeling his presence across the room would still be uncomfortable, it would certainly be easier than having him so physically near and hearing his voice.

Just then she felt Rairai gently slip his arm around her waist, as he politely laughed at something Bitterridge had said. It was only part of the role he was playing, but at that moment, it was also a pleasant distraction. To get through tonight, Atira knew she would require distractions.

CHAPTER 49

She felt tired as she stared at herself in the large opulent gold-framed mirror. The mirror was a lavish piece that she would have had the people downstairs sell for food and clothing had it not been built into the wall by those wealthy Lessers who had occupied her house. Removing it would have left behind a mess and a large gaping hole.

Atira found herself now focussing specifically on the gold shimmering gown she was still wearing. It was a unique dress she had found in a small laneway shop. She chose it because its color and shimmer were very much like that of the beautiful lakes on her home world. It was also a perfect fit, draping over her shoulder, around her waist then gracefully hanging down over the curves of her hips. She couldn't have found a better choice for the party.

Oh, the party and Zylong... What was it he thought he saw when he looked at her? All through the evening, she kept noticing him staring from across from the room. She knew that look well. It was a look she had once mistook for love, but now knew what it truly was. It was hunger. Base empty self-serving hunger. The kind of hunger that Moloch thrived upon.

She reprimanded herself for allowing him to enter her thoughts again, then abruptly turned from the mirror. Now, she faced her console where dozens of screens were open and active, operating automatically because of the recent algorithms sent by her Naomh. Just the thought of her Naomh made Atira sigh with longing. With all her heart, she wished at that moment she could hear his voice again and not simply receive codes and vague instructions from light years away. But she knew this was not possible yet. She'd have to complete the mission first. This was necessary to trick Moloch. She knew the beast had sensed her presence on the planet since the moment she had first arrived, and if it heard her Naomh talking directly with her, it would root itself even deeper into the world and try and hunt her down. Keeping her communication with her Naomh a secret was important to the mission.

Just as she decided it was best to now prepare for bed, there was a soft knock on the door. It surprised her as it was very late for anyone in the house to be awake. "It's me," said Taqwi from the other side. "May I come in?"

"Come in," she replied, a little worried this late-night visit could mean there was some sort of trouble in the house.

Taqwi slid open the door and stepped inside. For a moment he was silent as he caught sight of the frantic activity on the console with its screens opening and shutting, displaying endless images and calculations. He had never seen it do that before. He then looked over at Atira and couldn't help being struck by how beautiful she looked in the gold dress. "I…I heard you come in and I just wanted to see if…if it all went well this evening. You walked right into the midst of the Noblatjs."

Atira was relieved there was no problem. "I've done it before, Taqwi," she said, wanting to share this with him. It wasn't fair Rairai knew something about her that he didn't.

"Really?" Taqwi was very surprised to hear this. He couldn't imagine Atira having walked among them and not raising their suspicion. Were they unable to sense that unusual presence about her?

"Yes, I have been among them before, but they don't know anything about me. From what I can tell, they only believe that I am the kind of woman who latches onto wealthy Lessers. It has served me."

Taqwi was amazed anyone could think such a thing. How could

they not see…not sense how complicated she was? "What wealthy Lessers have you known?" he asked, then quickly worried that it might be an offensive question.

If it were asked by anyone else, Atira might have taken offense, but this was Taqwi, and she knew he was not like that. Not wanting to hide anything from him, she answered, "His name was Zylong. It was a mistake…a mistake I regret."

"I know of Zylong," said Taqwi, surprised. "Were you helping him, like you are helping Rairai?"

Atira thought about how she would answer this. Both her instincts and intellect told her that it was best to be as truthful as possible. "At first, I suppose I was…helping him. He seemed lost… confused…in need of help. But then, before I knew it, it turned into something more… it turned into something else. Like I said, it was a mistake. It's finished now."

Taqwi could see it hurt her to talk about it. "I appreciate your honesty with me," he said, not wanting to pry further. There were things from his own past he wouldn't want to speak too much about, so he understood.

As he was about to leave, Atira surprised him by saying, "Sit down a moment," gesturing to two chairs near the window. "I'd like to explain some things to you."

"Alright," he said, as he walked over then waited for Atira to sit in the chair opposite before he sat down.

For a moment, the two simply sat together in silence. Atira wanted to fully sense his presence, before deciding exactly what to tell him. She looked into his kind eyes. They were honest and reflective of an open heart. Taqwi was very much a sincere and a good man. Her Naomh had told her, that when she met an alien, one she knew she could really trust, and one who was both open and willing, it was permissible to reveal some of the secrets. In her weakness, she had revealed things to Zylong, but only a little. Even when they had mind-merged, there was always that gut feeling…a warning she didn't quite understand at the time. She now knew it was her instinct telling her to hold back. She had never told him she was from another planet or revealed the extent of her powers, although she knew he suspected something.

Now, as she sat here with Taqwi who had proven himself over and over again to be a man of integrity, she felt no deep warning inside of herself, only a sense that this alien sitting across from her could be trusted.

"I'm not from here," she began, "from this planet."

Taqwi smiled, knowingly. "It's common knowledge that there are aliens somewhere out there…in space, and I assumed you were from another world," he said. "The things you do, the things you say, and that." He pointed to the console. "I simply thought it was best not to ask…to wait for you to tell me if you wanted to."

Atira smiled back at him. "Yes, my world is far away from this one."

"So, what are you doing here? Why bother to come to this forsaken planet with all its problems?" he asked.

"That is precisely why I am here," she said. "This planet has great problems. It needs to be fixed and I know how to do it."

This made Taqwi smile even more. He already knew why she was here, he just wanted to hear her say it. "Can it be done? Can you actually fix this world?"

Atira sighed and stared over at the console. "Moloch," she said. "It's about defeating Moloch."

"Moloch?" Taqwi was surprised to hear that name. "That's the mythical evil beast the old temple people speak of. Not many believe in him anymore. Just a few who still cling to the old ways."

"Moloch is real," explained Atira. "But he is not one being and not even a 'he'. Moloch is many in the disguise of one and it spreads its tentacles throughout the universe. It wraps itself around worlds and strangles the life from them. It is the mission of those like me to visit worlds and cut off these tentacles before they destroy everything. Moloch nests within power systems that oppress, steal and murder. It recruits servants and lays eggs to increase its control and make itself stronger and more capable of taking over other worlds. Because it exists within the shadowy folds of this dimension, you cannot see it. You can only know it by what it does in a world…how it reaches in and twists everything into something dark and horrible."

Taqwi closed his eyes for a moment. It was terrible to think that the old legends about Moloch were somehow true. Those old stories had frightened him as a child, and now they were frightening him again. He didn't want to believe it, but he had to accept that what he was hearing was real. Shying away from the truth was never a part of who he was. That was for cowards. Long ago he found freedom when he accepted that the Noblatjs were fakes, and now he must accept this truth to continue to move forward. "So, the Noblatjs, are they a part of Moloch?" he asked, as he opened his eyes.

"Yes and no," she replied. "Their unchecked greedy desires and arrogance have given a home to Moloch. They are like the bindings that hold the nest together. The bindings must be broken, and the nest must be disassembled. Only then can Moloch be stopped."

Taqwi was astounded by what she had just told him. To think there was a hidden reality that neither the Noblatjs nor the Lessers knew anything about…an unsettling reality. And even though, what Atira had told him was frightening, it also gave him hope. It meant change was possible. If this place with all its injustice and oppression could be made different…better, he wanted to have a hand in it. Leaning in closer to her, he said "Of course you know I will help you in anyway you require. You only need tell me what to do."

Atira reached over and took his hand in hers. Taqwi felt a pleasant surge of energy course through his body, making him wonder about the extent of her alien powers. "You have taken care of the refugees," she said to him. "It would have been much easier for you to just walk away. You have the know-how to be a wealthy Lesser, if you desired, but instead, you choose to help the weak and the hungry. Taqwi, you are helping now, and were helping long before I arrived here. To find someone like you on a planet where Moloch has taken such hold is to find a great treasure. Whenever you are feeling a little overwhelmed by your responsibilities, remember that you are a treasure."

CHAPTER 50

Rairai stood staring at the glowing red zinco-door in front of him. It was made from pure polished zinco-rock found only on the highest mountain ranges of Fallzinia. It was the same kind of door Twydi always said he would have one day. Only the wealthiest Lessers could afford such a thing. It was a status symbol of the highest order...a dream door.

Earlier that day, he had been surprised when a message from Zylong appeared in his infolio. It simply said:

> Meet me for drinks, three moons past the second wave.
> My home. We have things to discuss.

At first, he felt flattered. The great Zylong had contacted him and even invited him to his home. But then he began to think more about it. Why would Zylong even bother with someone like him? Sure, he was a recent success, but he wasn't established enough or connected to a wider circle of Noblatj to be of any use to someone like Zylong. There had to be something more to it.

Before he could locate the buzzer, the door opened and a reliable looking maid in a tidy service smock cheerfully welcomed him, "Come in Mr. Swyer. He is expecting you."

Rairai stepped inside. He was shocked by just how grand the hall was. Although not quite as elaborate as the Noblatjs' homes he had seen in infolio-zine pictures, it was very close. The walls were made of oscillating lights that had an immediate and strange calming effect, and the floors seemed to ebb and flow like the soft blue waves of an ocean, making him feel comfortably dazed.

"This way please," said the maid.

Rairai followed her down a long hall to what he first thought was an outside terrace. But when he looked up, he realized that the sky was actually a three-dimensional image panel.

"Rairai, I'm so glad you could come! Please come in and sit down?"

Rairai, who had been so mesmerized by the realistic quality of the sky image, hadn't noticed Zylong lounging on an arro-bed at the far side of the room. He was shocked to see the arro-bed knowing that they were strictly forbidden to Lessers. "Uh…hello," he replied, not sure how he should address him since they only met briefly once before.

"Sit please," said Zylong, pointing at an over-stuffed chair opposite the arro-bed.

Rairai walked over and sank down into the soft blue velvet folds. Even though it was of the finest quality and designed for ultimate comfort, it did not make him feel comfortable. Instead, it only made him feel vulnerable.

"It was such a pleasure to finally meet you the other night, Rairai. I'm not sure why we've never had a chance to meet before. The world of us wealthy Lessers is not really that big. Anyway, we didn't get much of an opportunity to talk, so I thought I'd invite you over for us to get to know one another better."

Just then, the maid, who at some point had disappeared from the room, returned with a tray containing two glasses and a bottle of Rails Sloof, a drink reserved only for the Noblatjs. She set it down on the table near the arro-bed then turned and left the room.

Zylong sat up and poured the Rails Sloof into the glasses. "You must try it," he said, pushing a glass in Rairai's direction while enjoying the stunned look on his face.

Rairai leaned forward and reached for the glass. As he held it in his hand, he stared at the strange liquid with its multi-coloured swirls. "I've seen Lofty Bitterridge drink it before," he said. "I have always wondered what it tasted like."

"Try it," smiled Zylong. "You're going to love it."

Rairai looked at Zylong and then took a small sip. He almost choked on the bitter taste but managed not show it. "Yes," he lied. "It's very nice."

Zylong took a large swig from his own glass then smiled. "This is by far the best vintage I've ever tasted."

Rairai simply returned the smile and nodded, then held up the glass to the light and pretended to be admiring its contents.

"We should have met before. Two wealthy Lessers like ourselves. We should really have met before," said Zylong.

Glancing around the room, Rairai noticed that there were image-plates of Zylong mounted on every wall. Some of them were of him alone, but many were of him in the company of the highest Noblatjs.

Zylong noticed him looking. "I always travel with my own official imager to catch my good side," he laughed.

"You know a lot of Noblatjs," said Rairai.

"I know every one of them…well almost every one of them. The most important ones anyway."

Rairai began again to wonder why he was here. Someone as big as Zylong couldn't possibly need him for a business deal. Had he simply impressed the man? Was there some deal in the works Zylong wanted him to be a part of?

"The party the other night was wonderful, wasn't it? Was that your first Noblatj party?"

"Yes," replied Rairai. "Well…at least, the first one of that level."

"And that woman you were with…what was her name again?"

Oh, so that's it. "Her name is Atira," he replied, surprised that Zylong would actually pretend he didn't remember her name. Was he really that arrogant?

"I like you Rairai," Zylong told him, "and because I like you, I'm giving you this warning. Lessers like us must be careful of who we associate with. We don't want to keep company with people who will just drag us down. And she's the type…the type guys like us must avoid. Do you understand what I'm saying to you?"

Rairai knew he had to play this carefully. "In what way do you think she'd drag me down?" he asked.

"Her kind...they can't be trusted...they have their ways. Just when you think everything is fine, then WHAM! She could ruin it all for you."

"Well, I appreciate your advice," said Rairai.

"Good," responded Zylong, believing that he and Rairai had an understanding. "I knew you were a smart man and we elite Lessers have to help one another out. You've risen quite high in the ranks of wealthy Lessers and I wouldn't want to see you destroyed by such as her."

Rairai was unsure just how to respond to this, so he simply nodded and smiled.

"Now," said Zylong, "would you like a tour of my image-plates? I have quite a collection." He got up and started walking towards the far wall. "Over here is one of myself and the great Lofty Todi who, as you know, is no longer with us."

Rairai got up to follow him. On his way across the room he ever so discretely emptied his glass of Rails Sloof into a potted plant.

CHAPTER 51

A new screen suddenly popped up on Atira's console. It was Taqwi calling from the infolio she had given him. He looked distressed. "Atira, we need help, now!" he pleaded before the transmission abruptly ended.

Atira knew that Taqwi had gone out with two of the children that morning. The little ones needed new shoes and he thought it was best for them to go to the shops with him. "If there is any hope for them, they need to know how to deal with the everyday things of this world, and they can't learn that shut away in this house. Life has taught them how to survive homeless on the street, but now I must teach them another type of survival."

Quickly identifying their location, Atira realized they were in a shop that was quite a distance from the house. She was trying to contact Taqwi on the infolio, but he was not responding. It was obvious they were in danger, but how could she possibly get to them in time? Her mind was racing, and she felt her frustration growing. "I must reach them!" she shouted, bringing her fist down upon her console. Suddenly, there was a bright and blinding flash and, in an instant, she found herself in the middle of a Lesser shop. For a moment, Atira didn't understand what had just happened, but then suddenly she realized. Quantum travel! It was something she had dreamed about for a long time and now, it had finally happened.

"No, you don't understand! Please, let the children go!" shouted Taqwi's voice from somewhere in the back of the store.

Atira hurried back and saw Taqwi with his hands bound and two police officers in the process of binding the hands of the crying children. Off to the side a salesman stood with arms folded, a satisfied smirk on his face.

When Taqwi saw Atira standing there, his face lit up. Atira, seeing the extent of the faith he had in her, knew it was ultimately that faith which had made quantum travel possible. Her Naomh had told her many times over that true faith is the most powerful force in the universe. Solaplasm and other standard forms of energy were crude and ineffective compared to faith, but faith was rare and could not simply be produced on a whim. It was a hidden wellspring that required the perfect combination of strength, courage and devotion for it to manifest. When it does manifest, the effects are amazing!

Before the police had even noticed Atira, she took out her quantum-eraser and, in an instant, they and the salesperson vanished. The children immediately stopped crying and were now just looking around in confusion, wondering where their tormenters had gone.

Taqwi smiled as walked over to Atira. "Would you mind?" he asked, turning around so that she could free his hands. Using her quantum-eraser, Atira dissolved the electronic bindings.

Taqwi then turned to face her and said, "Thank you. I didn't know how we were going to get out of that."

The children came running over and she quickly removed their bindings also. Then, with a wave of her hand, short circuited and wiped clean the entire surveillance system both inside and outside the building.

"We were just shopping when the salesman decided he did not like the look of us...decided we weren't good enough for his shop," explained Taqwi, as he picked up his confiscated infolio from a nearby table. "I tried to explain that we had money to pay, but then he accused the children of stealing and called the police."

"We didn't steal anything!" exclaimed one of the children.

"Yes, you are not thieves," said Taqwi, "You are good children and I know that you did not take anything. The man lied."

Atira looked at the children. Their little eyes were still wet from crying and she could sense the pain and fear that had already filled too much of their lives. She wanted to make them feel glad and hopeful. "You are good children," she said. "They were bad men, but they are gone now. Look around the store and take whatever you wish."

For a moment, the children did not know if Atira was being serious, but then one of them laughed and excitedly began to run around gathering up clothes and shoes. The other followed behind. "I just told them they were not thieves," protested Taqwi.

"This world is built upon thievery," replied Atira. "All that you see in this shop has, in some way, been stolen from these children. I only return to the children what is theirs."

Taqwi could see there was no arguing with her. Later, he'd explain to the children how this was a unique situation and that they couldn't always act like that. "I'm just so happy you came," he said to Atira. "If we had gone to prison, the little ones would have been placed in work camps. I had no idea that I could just call you like that, and you would appear."

Atira watched with satisfaction as the children gathered up shoes and clothes in their arms. She could see that they were taking many things that did not fit...things for their friends back at the house. They were not acting selfishly. In their windfall, they were still thinking of others. This was good. "I wouldn't have been able to get here in time without your faith, Taqwi," Atira explained to him. "Faith is a power that changes everything. Remember that."

CHAPTER 52

"Zylong invited me for drinks."

Atira was facing her console when Rairai told her this. She turned to look at him. "It is the kind of thing he would do," she said.

"He warned me to stay away from you…said that you would ruin everything."

Atira sighed and shook her head. "And do you believe him?" she asked.

"I see the good you do here…with the children and the others. No, I don't believe him. I think he's jealous."

Atira turned back to the console. "I'm sure he was not happy when he found I had gone," she said.

Rairai walked over and stood at the side of her console so he could see her face. "Why did you leave him?" he asked. "Maybe you could have used him. I've been useful to you. Wouldn't he have been even more useful?"

Continuing to stare at the many panels open in front of her, Atira answered, "I am not allowed to be deceptive on that kind of a personal level, and my mission dictates that I must put my positive energies only into good people. Did you see anything good about him? When you were there, in his home, I suppose that he showed you all his image-plates of him posing with the Noblatjs, and I suppose he bragged about every one of them. At anytime in your visit did you see anything that would make you say, 'this is a good man who does good things'?"

"I don't even know if I'm a good man," Rairai replied with a sigh.

"The fact that you can even ask that question of yourself means it's possible. He cannot even ask that question of himself. His pride and arrogance prohibit it. He believes without hesitation that he is good."

"Did you care deeply for him?" Rairai asked, then wondered if his question was too personal.

Atira was silent for a moment then answered, "I care for everyone until they give me reason not to," as she opened a new panel on her console.

Rairai was about to ask her another question when suddenly she exclaimed, "Look here! Is this Twydi? He appears to be wearing that jacket...the one you came looking for."

Rairai stepped around to face the screen. "That's him! That's Twydi!" he shouted in excitement. Although he couldn't see the face of the man being dragged along by two security guards on either side of him, he knew it was Twydi...the jacket...the build of his body. He had no doubt this was him. Suddenly, Twydi lifted his head and seemed to look directly at the camera. There was blood running from his nose and his right cheek was red and swollen. His blackened eyes were the most telling with their pleading, desperate look. Rairai watched as the two men then brutally stuffed him into a hovercraft. It was the same type of hovercraft that Rairai had seen from the data pin he had taken from the Badlands...a hovercraft with Lofty Bitterridge's brand on the side. Rairai then watched as it drove away.

"This is security footage taken outside Twydi's apartment," explained Atira. "It had been erased, but my console has the ability to pick up the ghost signatures and restore it. Everything in this world leaves a ghost signature, but the Noblatjs do not know about it. They think they can hide their crimes and not be found out, but there is nothing they can hide...nothing that cannot be revealed."

Rairai was speechless. To have seen Twydi's body was emotional, but to see him there…his face battered, staring back at him with a look so full of fear and despair. This made it all too real. His legs felt shaky and he thought he might break down in tears.

"Do you need more?" asked Atira. "I could find you more, if you like."

"No," said Rairai, not wanting to see anymore. "That tells me all I need to know."

"What would you like to do about it?"

Gritting his teeth, Rairai replied, "I want to take down Lofty Bitterridge! I want to end him the way he ended Twydi!"

"Continue to help me," said Atira. "And, I promise, you will get your chance."

CHAPTER 53

Atira sat on a bench on the farthest side of the garden. She watched with contentment as the children ran and played, laughing and shouting happily. It was nice to get away from her console and see this. The children were a promise being fulfilled. *I am making a better world for you, but you cannot see it yet. Trust me, little ones. It is coming.*

"May I sit with you?"

Atira was so busy watching the children that she didn't notice Taqwi approaching. "Of course," she answered, happy to see his warm smile.

Taqwi sat down next to her. "I need to speak with you about something I have done," he said nervously.

"What have you done?" she asked, wondering what it could possibly be.

Taqwi stared guiltily at the ground. "I have spent everything that was in the infolio," he said quickly.

Atira was surprised. There was enough for several years of support on that infolio. "How could you have spent everything?" she asked.

"It was getting too crowded in the house. More and more were coming. I couldn't turn them away. Something had to be done." He kicked a small stone near his foot. "Also, people around here were starting to notice...all the children...all the comings and goings. Something had to be done."

"Just tell me please. Tell me what you have done."

"I bought up almost all of the houses on the street," Taqwi said quickly.

Atira could not believe her ears. She then started laughing. "You took all that money and bought all of the houses on the street? How did you do that?"

Taqwi sighed in relief. "I thought you might be angry."

"Angry? You did this for the children and for the others in the house. Why would I be angry? I am not here to take the place of the Noblatjs, I am here to free this world."

Without thinking about it, he reached over and took her hand in his. "I'm so glad. I'm so glad you're here," he exclaimed.

Atira felt the warmth of his hand and his words, and for a moment, she had an intense desire to mind-merge with him. Quickly, she dismissed this notion. She had already suffered too much from her mind-merge with Zylong and did not want to risk trying it again. Of course, Taqwi was nothing like Zylong, but she simply didn't feel ready to take that chance again. The mission required her complete focus so she must resist all temptation. Discretely pulling her hand back from his, she asked, "How did you convince them to sell to you?"

Taqwi laughed. "The sinkhole across the street. I frightened them into believing the same thing might happen to them. I told them I was an expert on the subject and wanted their homes for my scientific study. They were more than willing to sell to me at reduced prices."

Atira laughed again. This was such a pleasant surprise to find out Taqwi could be so resourceful and forward thinking. He was a better alien than she had ever hoped for. "Thank you," she told him. "This was a wonderful idea! You, of course, will be in charge of seeing to it that the houses are all well managed."

"I take full responsibility," he said happily.

"These people are in good hands with you," Atira replied. She then looked into his soft warm eyes and thought once more about mind-merging before quickly looking away. "We should go to my console and add to the infolio. I have additional funds already to load. They were a donation from a Noblatj," she said.

"A donation from a Noblatj?" laughed Taqwi.

"Come", she said, getting up and heading towards the house.

Taqwi jumped up from the bench and followed her. He was already thinking about more ways he could assist the growing community. In his wildest dreams, he had never imagined he would be building such a thriving little world. When he first found himself in the company of a group of homeless Lessers, he also found himself falling naturally into a leadership role. He didn't choose it. It simply fit. They accepted him as leader, and he was good at it. There were many hard times when he had struggled and despaired for his people, but there was always hope. As a committed leader, he always had hope. Now, however, he was filled with more hope than he had ever imagined possible, and it was all thanks to one woman who had opened her door and welcomed strangers in. As he followed Atira inside the house, all he could think was how he could follow her anywhere.

CHAPTER 54

"You know that will solve nothing," Atira said to Rairai as she sat in the chair by the window. "If I were to dissolve Lofty Bitterridge, he would simply be replaced by another Noblatj. Their laws prevent you from ever properly owning your company. Also, my own laws prevent me from doing this."

Rairai paced back and forth. Recently he had been having nightmares about Twydi, and the anger was now growing inside of him. Thoughts of getting rid of Lofty Bitterridge, once and for all, were beginning to consume him. "But what can I do? Some days I don't know if can go on like this! It's so frustrating! Couldn't you break the rules just once and zap him with that...that thing? Maybe the next Noblatj will be different."

"It would not be different, and you know it. In all probability, it would be worse, and you will continue to find yourself in the same servitude as you do now. Do you want to spend your life waiting and wondering when Twydi's fate will also be your own? Heaven Sent is a lie. Twydi knew this and that could be why he was killed. He was a threat to the secret, and you too will eventually be seen as a threat. Walking away isn't even an option. They wouldn't let you walk away with such knowledge. They'd kill you first."

Rairai realized that Atira was right. All available choices seemed to lead only to his doom. "How am I to get out of this?" he pleaded. "There has to be a way."

"There is only one way," Atira said. "We must change everything."

"What do you mean change everything?" he asked.

"The entire world. Everything. The order has to change."

Rairai shook his head in disbelief. "How? How could you possibly change this planet? The order of things is entrenched. The Noblatjs have ruled for as long as can be remembered and we have always served them. You really think you can change that?"

"I am going to change this world," Atira said confidently. "Are you ready to support me?"

Rairai didn't know what to say. For him, hope and faith had never played much of a part. He had always relied on pragmatism. Pragmatism was security. Whenever things went bad, he knew that, if he kept a realistic perspective, this would be enough to carry him through. All he really wanted was the immediate satisfaction of destroying Bitterridge. The idea that anyone could alter the entire power structure of the Noblatjs seemed ludicrous. "How can I promise to support something that seems so impossible?" he asked her.

"What choice do you have?" replied Atira. "You know you cannot live without getting justice for Twydi and I am telling you that justice will be delivered. And not only will there be justice for Twydi, but there will be justice for your entire planet. What do you have to lose by supporting me?"

Rairai thought about it. What did he have to lose? His choices in life had boxed him completely in, and he needed a miracle to escape. Could Atira make that happen? He had seen her do things he didn't think were possible. Could she do this too? "I suppose you're right," he relented. "I've really got nothing to lose. And things definitely can't go on the way they are so, I'll make you this promise...I'll support you anyway you need. Just let me know what I must do."

"I will not need much from you," she said. "Just continue to protect this house and keep our secrets, and when the time comes, you will have a role to play."

"And you promise that Bitterridge will be destroyed?"

"That," she said, "will happen. You simply must be patient."

Patience. "Be patient, Twydi," he used to tell his friend all the time. Now it was him. He was the one who had to have patience. Even if he couldn't bring himself to believe that the world could change, he could at least muster up the patience to believe that one way or another Bitterridge would get what he deserved.

CHAPTER 55

"What are we doing here?" Taqwi asked as he looked around the opulent lobby. "You said we were going to pick up food."

Atira smiled at him. "Yes, we are here for food…a different kind of food."

Taqwi was even more confused. What exactly were they doing at the Ministry of Noblatjs Social Affairs? He was feeling very nervous that at any moment one of the many guards would become suspicious and they would be arrested.

"There is a room on the lower level," she said. "What we need is there. That is where they have hidden it."

Taqwi didn't ask any more questions, but instead silently followed her to the cyber-lift. As the lift door closed in front of them, a surprising wave of emotion overwhelmed him. At first, he thought it was anxiety, but then he realized this was something else. It was excitement…a unique unusual electric excitement that he could only remember feeling once before. As a child, he was riding his turbo-rider, a shiny new red one…a birthday present from his grandmother. Earlier that day, he had been adjusting the speed-compass in the childish hopes of turning it into a time machine. Somehow, he accidently managed to unlock the speed-restrictor and found himself rocketing across the empty fields. At first, he was frightened, but then all he could feel was the euphoria of absolute freedom.

He screamed with delight as he flew over and around everything in his path. At one point, he even did a perfect air loop, swooping up several feet in the air and then coming back down in a faultless arc. Later, when he returned home, it was discovered that he had burned out the engine. Because of this, he was told he would not get another turbo-rider, but Taqwi didn't care. It had been enough just to have experienced such joy that one time.

The cyber-lift door opened, and they stepped out into a drab ordinary hallway. It was quite a contrast from the opulent area they had just left.

"Do not worry about cameras," Atira told him as they carefully moved along the long and winding corridor. "From my console, I was able to adjust the system so it would not reflect our images. We are invisible."

"And voices?" Taqwi asked.

"It does not pick up those either. We are ghosts."

Taqwi liked the idea of being a ghost. Moving through those corridors of power with no one able to see him...no one able to stop him. Above them, the Noblatjs were going about their business completely unaware of what was happening below.

"Could you not have simply appeared here, like you did when we were in trouble in the shop?" he asked her.

"It was your faith and my urgent desire to reach you that made it possible. Quantum travel is not something that can be wished for. Certain pure energies must be in place for it to work. It is very complex but, thanks to you, now that I have experienced it, the door is open for it to happen again when the circumstances are right."

Taqwi considered asking about what kind of circumstances were needed, but decided it was better to focus on the task at hand. "So why are we here and what are we looking for?" he asked.

"To be honest, when we started out this morning, I had no idea we would be coming to this place. My instincts, having become much more finely tuned in the recent weeks, guided me here. They told me that what I need is hidden in this building. As we get closer to our goal, those same instincts will help me know what it is I am looking for."

All this talk about energies and the power of instincts reminded Taqwi that Atira was still very much an alien, and that he should never assume he understood everything about her. Although some days it felt like he knew her very well, she was always revealing new things about herself. He should never take anything she said or did for granted. She was unlike him or anyone else on this planet, and he needed to remember that.

"It's here," she said, stopping in front of a non-descript gray door. "I can feel it and I now understand what it is."

Taqwi reached over and pushed the button. The door immediately slid open. "It isn't locked?!" he exclaimed with surprise. "Why wouldn't it be locked if there is something extremely valuable inside?"

"For the simple reason that arrogance is a form of willful stupidity," she told him. "This room contains the truth...the indisputable truth. They do not secure this place because they do not want to even accept that the truth exists. They have grown so complacent believing in their own lies and power, that they no longer even guard against their greatest threat. Remember Taqwi, the ignorance within arrogance is one of our greatest weapons against the servants of Moloch. We rely upon their foolishness. Now let us get what it is we came for."

CHAPTER 56

A tira was busy at her console working on her multi-faceted dis-tribution plan. The important secrets she and Taqwi had found in that basement needed to be handled very carefully. There was a serious risk that the Noblatjs could shut down the entire communi-cation system before there was total revelation. So many safeguards needed to be installed and new pathways needed to be opened. The truth must be protected from all suppression.

Just as she was meticulously tracing the branches of the core network, her concentration was broken by the sound of loud voices coming from outside. Atira got up and walked out onto the balcony to see what was happening. When she looked down at her front entrance, she was in shock. There was Zylong and an unknown female wealthy Lesser shouting and pounding on her front door.

"Do you know who we are? We demand to be let in!" screeched the woman. Atira couldn't see Zylong's face from that angle, but she knew him well enough to know he was smiling. Making a scene at someone's door was the kind of thing he'd find amusing. She used to see this as a sign of a rebellious carefree heart but came to realize it was only about his vanity and childish need for drama. Although he sometimes played the part of the rebel for the Noblatjs' amusement, he never did anything truly rebellious. He never did anything he didn't feel completely safe in doing.

Atira could hear one of the women from downstairs open the door and tell them to go away which only seemed to agitate Zylong's companion even more. "Who are you to tell us to go? This is Rairai's house and we are his friends. Let us in!" She then watched as the wealthy Lesser pushed her way through. Zylong followed after her.

Hurrying to the stairs, Atira rushed down. She had to stop them from entering further into the house. They were still standing near the front door, when she reached the bottom and blocked their way.

"Well," smirked Zylong. "Look who it is. Do you know who this is?" he asked his companion.

The woman looked Atira up and down and said, "She's not much to look at, now is she?"

Atira glared at Zylong. How could you? How could you come here? How could you bring this woman into my house?

Zylong saw the hurt on Atira's face and for a moment felt bad for coming. But he quickly shook off this feeling. He now stared curiously down the hallway where the woman who answered the door had disappeared. He wondered what was down there and thought he heard the noises of children coming from somewhere inside.

"Are you Rairai's umm… friend?" giggled the woman.

"You are not welcome here. Leave!" demanded Atira.

The woman laughed at her. "Oh, how rude!" she chided. "We came all this way to visit Rairai and you would throw us out? That's highly uncivil of you to want to cast us out like we are some sort of homeless Lessers. It's not even your house. It belongs to Rairai."

"This is your last warning, now leave!" Atira could feel her anger rising and didn't know how long she could contain it.

"Maybe we'd better go," said Zylong who was again having second thoughts about coming. He could sense Atira's rage and it left him feeling unsettled.

"No, I'm not leaving," declared the woman. "I want to see this house. And what are those sounds? Are they hiding something here? I'm sure Lofty Lyon would be very interested if there is something illegal going on."

"Take her outside!" Atira demanded of Zylong.

"Who do you think you are, Lesser, to demand that I should leave!" sneered the woman. "I am one of the Noblatjs' favorites. I am also extremely wealthy? And who are you? Only some nasty little gigi-girl trying to move up the ranks. When my Noblatj friends hear how you have treated me…"

"Come on, let's just go," interrupted Zylong and taking her arm to leave.

"No!" shouted the woman, pulling her arm away. "I refuse to be treated like this and by someone like her. I intend to see what's going on in this house. She's obviously hiding something." She then darted around Atira and started down the hallway.

Before she could get far, Atira rushed her and pinned her up against the wall. Now unable to move under the pressure of Atira's arm, she went silent in shock. How could someone so much smaller than herself be so strong? The woman was now helpless.

"Atira, no!" shouted Zylong afraid of what might happen next.

Reaching into her pocket, Atira secretly took out her quantum-eraser, but before she activated it, she remembered what she had been taught, *Emotions are power, but without reason they become weakness.* Quickly, she thought about how she couldn't let Zylong know about her weapon but also couldn't disintegrate them both without raising the suspicion of the authorities. Being at such a crucial point in her work, it would be too risky to add such complications. Instead, by setting it at the lowest setting, she could simply damage the woman's brain. It would begin with confusion and forgetfulness, and then, over a period of a few weeks, she would appear to expire naturally.

As the woman angrily opened her mouth to protest, Atira discretely placed the quantum-eraser against the back of her head. She activated it and the woman's tense body suddenly slumped beneath her arm. Releasing her hold, Atira took three steps back. The woman, no longer combative, was now leaning silently against the wall, gazing into space.

"Josuk!" exclaimed Zylong. "Are you alright, Josuk?" The woman did not answer.

"Josuk!" he exclaimed louder and hurried over to her.

"I want to go," the woman muttered. "Take me home, Zylong. I'm so tired."

For a moment, Zylong just stood there in confusion. He then took her gently by the arm. She leaned against him for support and mumbled, "Let's go. I want to sleep."

Zylong looked over at Atira. "What happened? What is wrong with her?"

Atira ignored his questions, walked over to the open door and exclaimed, "Get out! Take her, get out of here and don't ever come back!"

The woman rested her head against Zylong as he helped her towards the door. He stopped near Atira and asked, "Did you do something to her?" His voice was trembling slightly.

Atira refused to even look at him as she said, "If you come back here again, I will not hesitate to kill you and anyone you bring with you. You know I can do it. You know that much."

Zylong did not say anything more. Instead, he simply guided his companion outside. As soon as they were across the threshold, he heard the door slide shut behind them and the locks activate.

"The sun is too bright," mumbled the woman who had now started to drool on Zylong's shoulder. "I need to sleep. Just let me go to sleep please."

Zylong felt sick. "Don't worry, Josuk," he said. "Let's just get into the hovercraft. Come on now. Do you see the hovercraft? We're almost there. You can make it."

"No!" she shouted and then began to weep uncontrollably. "I'm tired. I'm tired. I'm…" her head fell forward, and she was now silent.

Zylong helped her into the hovercraft then turned to look at the house one last time before getting in and driving away.

CHAPTER 57

Taqwi had gone out that morning in search of the three children Atira told him were begging at the base of a Noblatj tower. Prior to this, he had spent two weeks searching for them but with no luck. By the late afternoon, he had finally spotted them rummaging through some rubbish outside of a restaurant. It was a relief to find them still alive. After buying them a meal and questioning them, he discovered that they were, in fact, alone. Their mother had gone out for food and never returned. They didn't know how long they had been surviving on the street and didn't require much convincing to follow him back to the sanctuary.

When he arrived at the house, with his charges in tow, Taqwi was looking forward to introducing them to Atira but she was nowhere to be found. He asked around and was told about the altercation with some wealthy Lessers who had shown up at the door.

"Where is she now?" he asked in concern.

"She's outside in the garden. She said she wanted to be alone," replied one of the women.

Taqwi left the children with the women and went outside to look for Atira. Not seeing her in the open section of the garden, he walked in the direction of the trees at the back of the property. As he searched through the wooded area, he suddenly caught sight of her colorful dress. She was turned from him and leaning against a large tree.

He walked up behind her and softly spoke her name. "Atira?"

When she turned to look at him, he was surprised to see she had been crying. Taqwi had never imagined this alien woman could cry.

Atira saw him noticing that she had been crying and quickly turned away.

"I came to find you," he said. "I was told about the man and woman who were at the house. Is everything alright? Who were they?"

Atira took in a deep breath and replied, "It was only Zylong."

Taqwi was immediately concerned. "Zylong? What was he doing here?"

"He saw me in the company of Rairai at the party, and I suppose, came here out of curiosity. I never thought he would have shown up at the house."

Taqwi moved around to face her. She did not turn away this time. "Does he present a danger to us?" he asked. "Would you like me to do something?"

Atira smiled at Taqwi's sincere concern and his offer. "Don't worry. He is no threat," she assured him. "I made it clear that he must not return, and I don't believe he will. He really knows nothing about me or this house, and if he has suspicions, he won't reveal them. Zylong has an intense fear of upsetting the Noblatjs with things that are of no concern to them. In his mind, I am still small and insignificant next to his beloved Noblatjs. His own arrogance and unquestioning belief in them work to our benefit."

"If it's not too personal, can I ask why you were crying? I did not even know you could cry, and it's none of my business, but I do care about you, Atira. You've built us such a wonderful place here. I purchased two more houses this morning, just inside the gates, and already they are filling up with displaced Lessers. In two more days, we will officially own this entire neighborhood and will be able to close those gates for our protection. This is your doing."

Looking at the ground, she gently stirred some auburn leaves with her purple shoe. "Thank you, Taqwi," she said. "You've shown me nothing but kindness. I've been to many worlds and met many aliens, and you don't know how rare it is to find someone like you. On my planet, we have a word for people like you. The closest translation would be: *those who bring unseen gifts that echo throughout the universe.*"

It made Taqwi happy to hear her say those things about him, but he was still concerned about her sadness. It didn't seem right that she should be feeling so sad. "Things are working perfectly for the community," he told her, "so why were you crying? Maybe I can help. I hope you feel you can be honest with me. You can tell me anything. Sometimes, it's necessary to talk about what is troubling you. I'm a very good listener. That's how I spend most of my days…just listening. I'm an expert at it."

Atira sighed. Taqwi was right. She needed to unburden. These emotions were taking a toll, making her weaker and putting the mission at risk. Taqwi was an honest man with honest intentions and she knew she could trust him. It was time to find some relief by sharing this with another person. Still looking down at her shoes, she said, "My Naomh, the one who sent me here, told me not to attach myself to things of this world. Just complete my mission and leave. But when I arrived here, the first thing that hit me was the stark empty loneliness of this place. It was so full of the echoes of pain and division, and I was so far away from home where such things do not exist. The intensity of the loneliness just seemed to be collapsing in upon me. In worlds like this one, where Moloch has taken such hold, negative feelings easily become more intense and especially feelings of loneliness. This was the first time I had ever experienced a planet that was this badly infected by Moloch.

So, I tried my best to forget about the loneliness and focus on the mission, but then without realizing what I was doing, I lost my way. Lured in and then deceived by my own hungry heart, I attached myself to something…to someone I should not have."

"Zylong?"

"Yes," replied Atira. "At first, I accepted his company only so that I could learn more about this planet and perhaps to help a confused alien along the way. I'm not even certain how it happened…my attachment to him. None of it makes any sense."

Taqwi reached out and briefly touched her arm. "Don't feel bad about that. We don't always choose our attachments. The heart can be like a wild uncontrollable beast that goes wherever it will. Who can understand its mysteries?"

Atira felt the genuine kindness and sympathy within his touch and in his voice. It was so much more than she had come to hope for from this place. "I did not ask much from him," she went on to explain. "I saw he was on the wrong side...I saw how wrong he was about a lot of things, but I didn't make demands or turn away. I wanted only to help him. Quickly, he saw my growing attachment and sensed my power. He decided to try and exploit me...to try and use me to his advantage. That's the worst part. He could have simply walked away, but instead he pulled me in further...deceived me in order to try and bolster his power among the Noblatjs. That I cannot forgive.

And today, he shows up here with some cruel arrogant woman...a valued servant of the Noblatjs. She tried to push her way into the house, but I stopped her then silenced her for good. I think that frightened Zylong and made him realize that he must keep his distance. It was obvious that he believes this is Rairai's house and that I am here only because Rairai is a wealthy Lesser. That is what he believes I am. He doesn't know about the community or all the houses or all the other Lessers. He doesn't know about my mission. We will not have to worry about him, Taqwi. The community is safe. You needn't be concerned about that."

"And what about you?" asked Taqwi. "I can see how hurt you are. It was painful for you when he showed up like that, wasn't it?"

"I am fine," said Atira, now feeling much better. "I have been to many worlds and endured many things. This is just another thing to be endured."

"If he comes around again, I'll..."

Before Taqwi could finish the statement, Atira interrupted him. "I don't believe he will. And now it's time for me to dry my eyes and put my focus back on the mission. Tomorrow, the community will be even larger, and it will not stop growing. Weeks ago, I promised you, Taqwi, that I would change this world…that you would have a better planet. I will fulfill my promise. Let's go into the house and discuss some of the plans to be put into place." Atira began to walk back towards the house.

"Wait," said Taqwi.

Atira stopped and turned to look at him.

"I…I wanted to say that if you ever feel an attachment to me," he told her. "It would not be a bad thing. I just wanted you to know that."

Atira smiled and then she did something that surprised him. She kissed him on the lips.

"If I ever feel an attachment for you, I will be a very lucky woman," she said, then turned and headed back towards the house.

Taqwi followed after her. He wasn't certain exactly what he was feeling at that moment, only that it was something very good.

CHAPTER 58

A tira hesitated as her finger hovered over the icon on her console. All the data she had found in that non-descript room at the Ministry of Noblatjs Social Affairs was waiting there to be released…a yet to be detonated bomb. If she did this, she knew everything would change. But that's why she was here. That's why she had travelled all those light-years to get to this planet. Her mission was to purify a world that had gone so terribly wrong.

She thought about her Naomh and how much faith he had put in her. Atira wished she had that much faith in herself. What if she had it wrong? What if she misunderstood something? Miscalculated? Let her ego and her pride distort things? Hadn't she made a horrible mistake with Zylong? What if she was missing something now as she had missed all the signs then?

Suddenly, she heard the sweet sound of Meebelle's voice downstairs. Many of the children had moved to other houses but Meebelle insisted on staying with Atira. "I must stay here because I want to be with Atira." When Taqwi told her what Meebelle had said, her heart had leapt with joy. Didn't Meebelle deserve a future?

And then there was Taqwi. What a good and honest man he was. He certainly deserved a better world.

Even Rairai who, despite his somewhat selfish ways, also deserved better.

I must face it. I can no longer let this go on. All doubt must be dispelled. I know what I am doing. I was very careful in my calculations. Any mistakes I made in the past are inconsequential to the future of my mission. I must not dwell on them...allow them to hold me back. My Naomh trained me well and believes in me still. If he did not, I would not be here. Moloch must be stopped on this planet and I am the only one who knows how to do it. It is now time to unleash one of the greatest powers in the universe...the power of truth. With that she pressed down on the icon, and even though there was nothing but silence afterwards, she thought she could hear the world outside exploding in chaos.

CHAPTER 59

Rairai was sitting in an office in the Bitterridge Building, examining the month's numbers when he heard a commotion in the hallway outside. He slid open the door to see what was happening. People were rushing past him towards the cyber-lifts. "What's going on?" he asked as he grabbed one woman by her arm. He didn't know her name, but he recognized her face as an infolio spokeswoman for Heaven Sent.

She looked at him angerly. "Let go! I have to get home! We all have to get home!"

"Why? What happened?" Rairai asked, thinking it couldn't be a fire. There was no alarm.

The woman tried pulling loose from Rairai, but he was determined not to let her go until he learned more. "Please, just tell me what's going on."

"It's madness out there! Everything is falling apart! It's on the infolios!" she shouted at him. "It's all there! The truth! Now, let me go!" Although he still didn't get a straight answer, he released her anyway and she rushed off, disappearing into the crowd at the end of the hallway.

Rairai didn't follow everyone to the cyber-lifts. Instead, he turned and headed towards Lofty Bitterridge's office. When he reached the executive waiting area, he could see that the doors to the waterfall hallway were wide open. For security reasons, those doors were always closed.

There was no one behind the receptionist's counter and no sign of any guards. As Rairai walked cautiously down the hall, little blue fish tumbled down the bright pink water walls as if everything were perfectly normal. When he reached the ram's head doors, for some reason, he didn't bother with the ringer. Instead, he simply pressed on the opening mechanism and it opened. This too surprised him as these doors were usually kept locked at all times.

Inside the office, the light was very dim, but he could see Lofty Bitterridge sitting behind his desk, his long white hair looking flat and wet. "What is happening?" asked Rairai, ignoring all protocol for addressing a Noblatj.

Lofty Bitterridge laughed nervously. "Didn't you hear?" he replied. "It's the end of the world."

"What do you mean?"

"It's all here!" Lofty Bitterridge exclaimed, picking up an infolio from his desk and tossing it across the room. It whizzed by Rairai's head and crashed into the wall behind him. "Everything!" he shouted.

Rairai was still confused about what was going on, but he couldn't help thinking that whatever had happened, it had something to do with Atira.

Lofty Bitterridge slammed his fist against his desk with such force, Rairai wondered if he had broken a bone. "They all know." He was now no longer shouting, but almost whimpering...pathetically whimpering. "Everything...all of it is in the infolios for the whole world to see, and I have been told that it is somehow even moving through the crowds of Lessers who are too poor to even own one. There are so many of them...so few of us." He clasped his hands to his head in apparent anguish.

Rairai was still trying to make sense of it all. "What? What is in the infolios?"

Lofty Bitterridge laughed again. "Poor, poor Rairai. You thought you had made it big with your deception. Heaven Sent, the greatest invention ever! And Rairai Swyer, the genius rags to riches Lesser! Do you think I didn't know? From the very beginning I knew it was a lie you had brought to me that day. But that's all part of the game, isn't it? You believe in me and I'll believe in you, and then we pretend it's all good as we sell our little lie to the suckers. It's so much easier to sell a lie if you convince yourself to believe in it. But when it is exposed…well then…BOOM! The end. All gone. No more believing. No more Heaven Sent."

"They know the truth about Heaven Sent?" asked Rairai, knowing that such a thing would be very big news, but wondering why the entire world seemed to be in chaos because of it.

"They know the truth about everything! Ah, but no! It's not the truth! No! We are still the Noblatjs. We are better, smarter, faster! Our blood is pure! Anything it says differently on those infolios is the lie!" Lofty Bitterridge suddenly put both hands flat on the desk, stood up and leered with pure hatred at Rairai. "And so, what if they know? There is nothing they can do about it. This planet is still ours!"

Rairai now understood what must have been on the infolios. It was what Twydi knew all along and what he had come to know. The Noblatjs were a fraud. This entire planet was built upon nothing but lies. Now everyone knew the truth and the pressure that had been building up for centuries under the tyranny of the Noblatjs was finally erupting.

Rairai stared at the angry screwed-up face in front of him. So often, he had been afraid of that bleached white visage when it wore only its usual confident smarmy smile. Now, it was horrifying in its violence, like some vicious cornered beast from the depths of chaotic obscurity, preparing to devour him.

A blue neon smile suddenly sliced across Bitterridge's red mouth. "Of course, Heaven Sent is gone," he said. "But it was always going to go. I hung on to it for as long as I could. I even had to get rid of that fool Twydi. He had a loose tongue and had already let the truth slip to some unfortunate young lady. He had to be annihilated. In time, I was planning on getting rid of you also. It would have all been mine eventually, which is only right. It's the proper order of things."

As Rairai stared at the raised angry veins beneath the thin skin of Bitterridge's forehead, it suddenly occurred to him that this murderer likely had a weapon nearby. "So, you killed Twydi," Rairai said, trying to sound confident even though he was terrified. It was clear he was too far from the door to get out in time if Bitterridge had a globular gun. He'd be dead long before he reached safety. Without any other options, Rairai discreetly glanced around for something he could use to defend himself.

"Are you really surprised?" Bitterridge smiled. "I'm a Noblatj. The reality is that we are allowed to kill Lessers. It's in our laws…the laws Lessers don't know about. We just usually do it in secret so as not to cause an uproar among the masses."

"Because the Lessers outnumber you," Rairai said. "So, you keep it all secret. If they knew the truth, all those Lessers might rise up and demand justice…like they are doing now. That's what is happening outside, isn't it? There is a revolution going on." Rairai then noticed that, among a cluster of art objects on the left edge of the desk, was a tall shiny metal spear-like sculpture. If he could just reach it, he'd have a chance.

Bitterridge winced at the thought of the chaos going on outside. He then angrily shouted, "Numbers?! What are numbers? We are the Noblatjs! We are stronger! Our blood is pure! This is our planet! We do what we want!"

Rairai had cautiously been moving ever closer to the desk. He was now almost within arms length of the sculpture, but he was also now closer to Bitterridge. "Maybe we can fix this together. Find some way that this can be beneficial to the both of us. Let's sit down and see if we can come up with a plan…a deal," Rairai said, as he tried to calm the Noblatj.

Lofty Bitterridge glared at him and then that ugly confident smile suddenly ripped across his face again. "Lesser, you are finished," he said in a calm dry dead voice. "I can only see you as something in my way now. Had we not required slaves, we would have gotten rid of your kind altogether. That's all you are in this world…disposable slaves. The Noblatjs will persevere because we are superior. The rebellion will be crushed, and it will simply be a shame that you will not be alive to see our glorious victory." He then pulled something small and shiny from beneath the desk.

Rairai didn't have to guess what it was. He knew it was a globular gun. Quickly grabbing Bitterridge's wrist, he sharply twisted it, and sent that bright beam of lethal protein harmlessly into the ceiling. With his left hand, he picked up the sculpture and, with all his might, thrust it deep into Bitterridge's ear. The Noblatj made a strange animal grunting noise as blood oozed out into his white hair. His eyes then rolled back into his head and he went limp, falling behind his desk.

For a moment, Rairai just stood there in shock. He could not believe what he had just done. Did he really just kill a Noblatj? Peering over the desk, he could see Bitterridge's crumpled body on the floor, the sculpture firmly impaled in his ear, his hair matted in a growing pool of blood and his right-hand twitching in death spasms.

Slowly backing away, Rairai could feel his heart racing. Although he had fantasized often about killing Bitterridge, he didn't know how to feel now that he had actually done it. He had actually killed a Noblatj! A Noblatj! Suddenly he was worried. What if someone had seen him. He looked around the room to make sure he was still alone. There was no one else about.

He then looked back at the desk and thought about the body on the floor behind it. What if Bitterridge was right…would the revolution be quelled, and the old order restored…would the Noblatjs be just as powerful as ever? If that were true, there would be an investigation, and anyone found guilty of murdering a Noblatj would be sentenced to a slow torturous death. Rairai knew he had to get out of there before someone saw him.

Thinking quick, he picked up the globular gun that Bitterridge had dropped, tucked it into his pocket then ran out of the room and down the hallway towards the cyber-lifts. When he squeezed in with the last group of evacuees, he thought about what must be happening outside and how everyone in the world now knew the truth about everything. That included the truth about Heaven Sent. Surely, people would see him as a friend to the Noblatjs and a swindler who had sold them a lie. The world was exploding in pent-up frustration and anger, and they'd be looking for someone to blame. Because of this, he knew it wasn't safe for him anywhere…anywhere except maybe one place. If he were to stay alive, he knew he needed to make his way there as quickly as possible.

CHAPTER 60

Taqwi came running into the room. "It's happening, Atira! Everyone knows their secrets! All their secrets! It's chaos out there!"

"Did you shut the gates," she asked, as she turned her chair from her console to face him.

"The gates are shut and locked."

"Good. We cannot allow anyone to harm the community we have built. It will be important to the future of this planet."

Taqwi stepped closer to her. "I've often fantasized about a day like today," he said. "About the time when everything would come crashing down on the Noblatjs. But now that it's finally here, I can't help feeling unnerved by it all. How will we even begin to rebuild?"

Atira stood up and stared into his eyes. Her gaze was gentle, steadfast and calming. She then reached out and softly touched his cheek. "Do not be afraid," she told him. "It will be alright in the end. All that is happening now is what is necessary to fix this planet...to eradicate Moloch. If things were allowed to go on as they were, all life on this world would have been completely destroyed. Planets where Moloch is not eradicated will naturally implode. This is tragic enough, but in their implosion, they send Moloch deeper into the universe and infect other worlds. And even though what is happening might appear as destruction, underneath it all I have woven the invisible threads that bind. They are too complex to explain in spoken language, but please know that these threads will hold together the goodness on this planet. You and the community are the center where all the threads meet, and that's why you must be protected. You are the key to a world free of Moloch." She then took her hand away.

"I...I don't think I quite understand," Taqwi said, secretly wishing she would touch him again. "It just all seems so...so unreal."

"You don't need to understand everything right now," Atira replied. "All you need to know is that Moloch had knocked this planet off balance. Those in power had created a system of death and oppression designed to devour all that was good. That is what Moloch does. It unbalances things and destruction ensues. The universe requires balance and when something like this happens, it is a threat to everything else out there. That is why my mission has been so important...why my Naomh sent me here. I had to fix this before your world reached the point of complete annihilation and now you will play an important role in rebuilding this planet the way it should be."

Taqwi was silent. The thought that his world was deeply connected to the greater universe was a new idea. He had never imagined such a thing before. Like everyone else on his planet, he had been taught that they were on a single sphere that existed independent of everything beyond it...of the aliens who were beyond it. Yes, they knew there were others out there, but they were only aliens from other independent spheres. It was amazing to think that, on a deeper level, they were all one.

"What is next?" he asked. "How long do we wait inside the walls?"

"For the moment, we keep the gates closed and sit still while the chaos plays out. In a short while, we will reveal ourselves and begin to put things together. Except this time, things will be put together the way they should be...without Moloch."

"And what will my role be? You said that I am the key, but I don't understand. What does that mean?"

Atira gave him a soft warm smile that made his hands and feet tingle. "You, Taqwi, are the key. At first, I did not realize it, but after months of witnessing your leadership and experiencing your presence, I now know who you are…your nature…your purpose. The universe has created you to be the restorer. You will replace the death the Noblatjs brought to this planet with life. You will be a great leader, the kind of leader this world needs."

Taqwi didn't know what to say. A great leader? He had never in his life wanted to be the leader of anything. Even his leadership role in the community was only because he had fallen into it. They needed him and so he helped out, never thinking too much about it. The idea that he would become a world leader seemed absurd. "Are you sure I'd be right for the job? There must be more qualified people for that challenge. I'm only an ordinary homeless Lesser. What do I know about taking care of an entire planet?"

"And did the Noblatjs know how to care for an entire planet?" she asked. "Their leadership almost destroyed this world. Could you do a better job than them? Never tell me you are only a Lesser. There are no more Lessers, no more Noblatjs. That is gone. You, Taqwi, have shown yourself to be a true leader. You have all the qualities a leader should have, strength, caring, humility and a natural sense of justice. And you have proven yourself time after time. You have built a strong and fair community. There is no argument for you to make here. You are the most qualified. You will lead them. Your entire planet depends upon it."

Taqwi then heard the muffled sounds of explosions in the distance and felt suddenly afraid. Atira reached out and took his hand in hers. She looked into his eyes and said, "Look deep inside, Taqwi. There you will find a clear clean untapped well…a well waiting to renew…to refresh. All that you need is inside of you."

With her touch and those words, Taqwi felt a surge of power course through his veins. All fear vanished as the soft comfort in her eyes filled him with visions of possibilities. Could this be the beginning of the kind of world he had always dreamed about? And if this was to be his destiny, to lead a vibrant new planet-wide community, he'd have to step up and accept that honor with strength and with courage. Atira had been right about everything so far and her faith in him was something he had to take seriously for his own sake and for the sake of the community and his planet.

Taqwi was just about to say something, when suddenly he was overcome with a force so beautiful no words would ever be able to describe it. He was floating free…above himself…above everything. But he was not alone. Never in his wildest dreams did he ever imagine such a thing could exist. To feel so complete…so whole…a union within the realm of perfection. O' sublime joy! Pleasure beyond pleasure! We are…we are…we are…one.

A tira had not intended to mind-merge with Taqwi, but it felt like the time was right and so she did. Having left him sleeping in her room, she now turned her thoughts towards the chaos she had unleashed upon the world. She could feel it crashing in all around...a purging force. It was not an entirely comfortable feeling, but it made her feel free of Moloch...well, almost free. She realized there was one last thing to do. In her heart, she didn't really want to do it, but knew it was necessary. Although giving the gift of revelation to the alien population had mostly defeated the beast, Moloch could still find refuge in some small multi-dimensional opening, and there was only one such opening left on the planet...an opening she herself had accidentally caused.

Slipping out the back door, she secretly made her way through the gardens of the community to a far corner of the security wall. This section was obscured from view by bushes on both sides so she knew she would not be seen. With her quantum-eraser, Atira then created an opening large enough to fit through.

Once outside, she didn't see anyone around although she could hear a great deal of shouting in the distance. She then walked a little way before spotting an abandoned police hovercraft. Getting in, she turned it in the direction of the Noblatj seaside neighborhood and accelerated.

Along the roads, she saw all the signs of a full-scale riot. Everywhere there were broken and discarded things that had been pulled from shops and restaurants. Most of the people seemed to have now retreated into their locked homes, but occasionally she'd pass by a small group of looters. They didn't seem to notice or care that a police hovercraft was passing by. Once, someone did throw a large metal object her way, but Atira saw it coming and sped up just in time.

In the distance ahead, she could now see a great cloud of billowing black smoke in the sky. As she got closer, it was obvious that the entire Noblatj seaside neighborhood was on fire. But that wasn't where she needed to go. It was the place just outside this neighborhood…an area below the Noblatj houses, where a few elite Lessers had been given homes. This was where she needed to go to eliminate that one last potential refuge of Moloch…this was where she would find Zylong.

CHAPTER 62

Rairai bent down and picked up a broad brimmed hat that a pillager had left behind in the street. It was a ridiculous tall purple thing that might not even have been a man's, but he didn't care. He needed something to hide his face. There were so many angry marauders about and he, a co-conspirator with the Noblatjs, was an obvious target for their anger. Once so proud of how they displayed his image everywhere, he now regretted that fame.

As he hurriedly made his way along the abandoned street, Rairai noticed a large group of men up ahead marching brusquely towards him. Without a second thought, he quickly slipped through the broken door of a ransacked restaurant and crouched behind an overturned table. As they approached, he could hear them arguing in undiscernible voices. He waited, hoping they would move on, but to his horror, they seemed to have stopped outside of the restaurant. Had they seen him go in there? Were they now planning their assault?

Suddenly, one of them shouted, "Over there! Let's get him!" causing Rairai's heart to nearly leap out of his chest. In that moment, he thought for sure they must have seen him dart into the restaurant and were now coming to finish him off. Was this to be his end… horribly beaten to death by an angry mob?

As he closed his eyes and braced for the inevitable, he could hear the voices now moving farther away. They had gone off in another direction. They hadn't seen him after all. Rairai leaned his back against the table and sighed in relief. He still had a chance to get out of this alive. Pulling the brim of the purple hat down farther over his face, all he could think was that he had to get back to Atira...back to the house. She was the only one who could protect him. She was his only hope. He peered around the edge of the table to make certain the coast was clear, then leapt to his feet and made a run for it.

ALIEN ATIRA

When Atira turned the corner, and saw the house again, a strong sense of longing suddenly overwhelmed her. Memories came flooding back...memories so full of hope...so beautifully wrapped in a promise for a future...memories warm and comforting. What if I'm wrong? Maybe this doesn't have to be like this. What if he just doesn't know what he is doing? Perhaps if I explain everything to him, he would begin to understand. We could start again. Getting love right would also seal the dimensional rift...it would seal the rift and so much more. Should I give it one more chance? Is it possible to fix this with love?

But almost as soon as she had thought these things, she caught herself. Hadn't she fallen for that illusion too many times already? And now here she was, about to make the same mistake again. She couldn't allow these deceptive thoughts. No matter how much her heart ached for it to be true, she had to be honest. If she allowed those feelings to come back full force, they would undoubtedly put the entire mission in jeopardy. Atira could not let that happen. She must turn away from desire for the sake of the planet...for the sake of the entire universe.

Exiting the hovercraft, she marched straight up to the glowing red zinco-door. Without a moment's hesitation, she took out her quantum-eraser and instantly dissolved it, leaving nothing behind but an undefended gaping hole. She then headed right for the sea-view room where she was certain he would be lounging on one of his prized arro-beds. Where else would Zylong be as the world was falling apart?

When she caught sight of him, she paused for a moment. He looked so calm and peaceful as he quietly stared out at the sea. How many times did the sight of him deep in meditation fill her with such joy? And how many times had she joined with him on that arro-bed? It was on that soft rich fabric where they had first mind-merged. And now seeing him there, it brought back all those old feelings. *My lover in repose*, she used to call it whenever she secretly watched him like this.

Atira quickly shook it off and looked away. She was doing it again. The truth! She had to remind herself of the truth. Lover? You need to be able to love to be a lover. He was never your lover! She stiffened her spine and called out, "Zylong!"

He slowly turned his head, looked at her for a moment, then casually looked back out at the sea. "What are you doing here?" he asked, bluntly.

"Finishing it," Atira replied, trying to keep her voice from trembling.

Zylong laughed out loud. It was a cold mean-spirited laugh that she had never heard from him before. She knew this was the laugh he had always been hiding…the laugh she often sensed but fooled herself into believing wasn't there.

"You finished it, alright. Do you see what it is like out there? You did that, didn't you?" he said.

"It had to be done."

"What do you mean, it had to be done?"

"You wouldn't understand."

Zylong jumped up from the arro-bed and took two steps toward her. "Don't be so arrogant! Tell me what you mean!"

It was clear, he was now projecting his own faults onto her. This, Atira knew, was something many aliens did when confronted with the truth. Whenever they couldn't face the reality about themselves and their situation, they would accuse her of the very thing of which they were guilty. The sad part was that, had it not been for his arrogance and ambition, things would have been different. He would have been different. Atira regretted she had not been able to get through to him…help him to make this change, but now there was no time left for sympathy. That possibility had come and gone. "Your planet was diseased," she said. "Things had to change. For the sake of life here and for the entire universe, it had change."

"So, you are an alien! I suspected that all along. Who do you think you are to imagine that you can change my planet? Do you think that I wasn't fixing it? I had the help of some of the Noblatjs. They knew what they were doing to the Lessers was wrong. We were going to fix it together. We had plans!"

Atira felt herself getting angry now. She had seen this many times on other worlds. Those causing the problems would often assign themselves the role of problem-solvers as a way to ensure that things did not really change. "Fix it?! Your Noblatj masters were not going to help you fix it. Why would they when all the benefits they enjoyed were because of this stagnant system? All they would have done is reorganized it to increase their own power and wealth. Their supposed liberation of the Lessers would have completely enslaved the population. The people would have been even worse off! I knew their plans better than you! I knew *everything* about their plans!" she shouted back at him.

"You're wrong! The Noblatjs would have provided and the Lessers would've been grateful!" he yelled. "They would not have wanted for anything! They would've been better off!"

"That's not true," she shouted back. "What is true is that one of your Noblatj confidants, who you worship so intensely, had actually come to believe your gossip about me…that I had special powers and was perhaps an alien. In fact, he had already been making plans for dissection and had even been pricing my body parts. He planned to dismember me for profit. That is the kind of sick savagery you believe in."

"That's a lie!" Zylong raged. "I know who you're talking about and he's a good Noblatj who would never do such a thing. He only wanted to help."

"He's dead now anyway," Atira told him. "One of the first to die. Killed by his own house servant. A fitting end."

"Why are you telling me this?" he shouted more upset than ever.

Atira was suddenly reminded that, for this interdimensional door to be closed, it had to be done within the energy of peace. She needed to control her anger and settle her mind into a good place. Taking in a deep breath, she calmly replied, "Because it's the truth. And the Lessers wouldn't have been better off. The plan was ultimately to make them complete obedient docile slaves. They would have had no freedom. Oppression would have continued only worse. From birth to grave they would have been made to serve the Noblatjs. Never being allowed to think for themselves…to progress…to evolve beyond the Noblatjs' limited way of thinking. No progression. No change. That's a living death. The Noblatjs were death for this entire world."

Zylong turned away and stared out the window at the sea. "How could you just walk out on me after all I did for you?" he asked in a sulky voice.

Atira could not believe he would ask such a question. "What are you talking about?" she said. "What you did for me? Do you have any idea what you did *to* me? Mind-merging with you opened a door to Moloch. All the terrible things within your mind, which are a part of him, now threaten me, and that threatens the security of this planet and the entire universe."

"What's a Moloch? What are you talking about? You're not making any sense. You were jealous. That's all. You were jealous, angry and spiteful, and now look what you've done. The entire planet is a mess."

Atira wondered if the hope she had once seen in this man was ever real. "Do you have any idea what you had in me?" she asked. "Do you have any idea at all what our mind-merging meant?"

"It was fun. I have to say that," he said with a smirk.

"Fun!? Mind-merging is not a foolish game. It is a serious matter… it can open the door to love. Sometimes deep love. And I *loved* you," said Atira, choking back those words. "I loved you even though I came to realize that you don't have the capacity to feel love in any real way. And what you can't feel, you can't understand. Where I come from…on my world, love is everything. It's food and drink and air. Love is life. Love is the greatest power and it doesn't happen easily. Not that kind of love, anyway. It's sacred. I don't even know why this happened to me. None of it makes any sense. You, being a servant of the Noblatjs, and me, loving you the way I did? There is simply no explaining it. Hopefully one day I will come to comprehend what it means."

Zylong turned from the window and smiled at her. "You can love me again," he said. "It's not too late. It was nice, what we had. Remember how nice it was?"

Atira recognized that smile. It was the same fake smile he gave the Noblatjs when he was trying to sell them on a deal. She was disgusted to see him try and use it on her now. "No, it's too late to try again," she told him. "And I know the truth. My love would go nowhere. To put the power of love into someone like you is to waste a valuable resource. On my planet, love cannot be squandered on the loveless. It must be put in a good place. It's the planting of a seed. If it is not done in healthy rich soil, the seed is either wasted or creates a crooked mutated plant. I cannot give you love anymore. You are poor infertile soil."

"Come on now," said Zylong, moving closer to her. "We had such good times together. Don't you remember what it was like. It was so good…mind-merging…right here…we could do it again. And maybe…maybe…I do love you. Did you ever think of that? You are so wrong about me. I'm a man capable of great things and love is certainly one of them. Why don't we see where this can take us? Aren't we worth another try?"

The part of her that still loved him desperately wanted to believe what he was saying, but she quickly reminded herself that, above all, Zylong was an actor and parasite. Now that the old world of the Noblatjs was over, he was lost. He needed to find a new place to placate his ego. His pleas had nothing at all to do with love and everything to do with strategy and self-interest. The word love was only a tool of deception for a man like him. It had no real meaning.

"My heart is anchored in my mission now," she said. "And I must finish. You…you almost ruined everything. You almost destroyed this world."

Zylong began to get angry again. "What are you talking about? I was trying to save this world. You are the one destroying it. I mean, just look at it! Look out that window and see it burning! Who is the wicked one? Not me. It's you! Admit it, you're nothing more than an evil alien and a scourge on my planet!"

There was a time when these words would have cut deep, but time had allowed Atira to build up her resistance against such things. Now, she saw him as he was, a man of weaknesses, lashing out like a frightened animal. "You are so good at deception," she told him, "that you even deceive yourself. Look at you. Look at how much you enjoy your wealth…your privilege. Would you have given up even a fraction of that if it meant saving the world? Would you? You never wanted to save the world. You only wanted power and luxury. Things could have been so different, if only you were different. You could have helped me save this planet, instead of only trying to help yourself."

Zylong was furious now. "You have no idea what you are talking about!" he shouted. "How pathetic you are, clinging to that Rairai loser. Going from wealthy Lesser to wealthy Lesser. My friends were right! You're nothing but a dirty gigi-girl! That's all you are, and all you'll ever be!"

Atira sadly sighed as she pulled out the quantum-eraser. Pointing it at him, she looked once more into his eyes and remembered how, early on, he had shown such promise. He had come so close to love, but he was too shallow for it to take root. Now, he had moved past all hope. He was completely lost, and it was time to close that final door on Moloch. There was nothing more she could do.

A single tear rolled down her cheek. It would be the last tear she would ever shed for him. "What must be done, must be done," she said, then without any more hesitation, activated the weapon. It was an instant death, but for Atira it appeared to take forever as she watched every last one of his cells disintegrate before her eyes. When he was gone, and there was only an empty silent space in front of her. She remained perfectly still and waited. It was coming…she knew it was coming. Then suddenly, it hit her! A sense of peace…a strong formidable lasting peace. It washed over her like a purifying wave, and she knew the door of Moloch was now sealed tight. What had to be done, was finished.

As she turned and walked away, she sadly whispered, "Zylong, you had no idea what you had…what you could have had. No idea at all." Then, from that moment on, she vowed to forget him forever.

CHAPTER 64

Rairai pulled the hat down over his eyes and began to make his way through the large crowd that had gathered in front of a Noblatjs monument. It was one of countless monuments erected in tribute to the greatness and superiority of the Noblatjs. Lessers were encouraged to pay homage and even give donations. There was a small acceptance panel at the bottom of each where money could be transferred from their infolios. This particular monument had been designed by a very highly regarded Noblatj artist. Its overall appearance was that of a shining white humanoid, but void of any discernible human features. Molded from the finest telidite gold, it was meant to symbolize the purity and perfection of the Noblatjs.

Two men had thrown ropes around the monument's neck and were now expertly scaling the slippery surface. Once they reached the top, they began to chip away at the head with small heavy duty jeppo-lasers. Every time they seared off a piece, they'd throw it out to the crowd, causing a mad and furious scramble for the tiny pieces of gold.

"Tear it down! Tear it all down!" screamed a woman as Rairai quietly slipped by her. The street was narrow here and he was trying his best to stay to the thinner outer edges of the crowd.

Suddenly, a piece of gold that had been thrown with extra force landed with a plunk right in front of him. He froze as he stared at its strange mocking gleam on the dark dirty road. Before he could move away, the crowd on all sides pushed in. Some of them dove straight at the gold and began to wrestle on the ground at his feet. Then, from behind, more people pushed forcefully forward, knocking him onto the pile of struggling bodies. For a moment, Rairai was completely disoriented. There were screams and shouts as he felt himself being helplessly tossed around by the writhing mass beneath him. Desperately, his hand searched for a hard surface to push himself up, but it only slipped on a soft mound of belly, causing his arm to buckle and him to fall back down into the mess of flesh. Someone large was now pressing down on his left leg. As he struggled to pull it free, he felt someone small fall onto his back and roll off again. For a moment, he wondered if he was going to die right there…to drown in that sea of bodies.

Then suddenly, the weight that had been pinning his leg was gone. Both legs were now free. With his right hand, he felt around and found the firmness of the road beneath him. The bodies that had been crushing him on all sides seemed to be moving off. He pushed himself up and off the remaining people, then quickly got to his feet. Rairai stood there for a moment dazed and confused. He was now unsure which way he was facing and in which direction he should go.

"Do I know you?" said an old man who came up close to him and stared directly into his face.

At that point, Rairai realized he had lost his hat in the mayhem. He was now completely exposed. Putting his head down, he replied, "No, sorry," then tried to push past the stranger.

"But I'm sure I know you," insisted the man still blocking his way. "Wait! Of course, I know you! You're Heaven Sent! You're the one who gave us that Heaven Sent lie! You're with them aren't you! The Noblatjs! You're one of them, you dirty lepis-pig!"

"That's him!" exclaimed a woman who was standing nearby. "That's the liar! Rairai is his name. I'd recognize him anywhere!"

Now more people were staring directly at him, their eyes filled with anger. Terrified, Rairai reached into his pocket for the globular gun he had taken from Bitterridge but realized it had been lost in the tussle. He began to panic.

Someone caught hold of his shirt, but Rairai managed to pull free. He then began to push through the crowd, looking for an opening. Angry voices were following close behind him.

"LIAR! LIAR! LIAR!"

At one point, a young man suddenly blocked him and grabbed his arm, but he was stronger and managed to break loose. Luckily for him, most of the crowd were so focussed on the destruction of the monument and the gold being tossed out that they barely noticed him pushing by.

Finally, he reached the edge of the crowd and from there broke out into a run. Not far behind, he could hear people shouting at him to stop. To Rairai it sounded as if there were hundreds in pursuit, even though he knew this couldn't possibly be true. He was tempted to look back, but instead kept his eyes focused ahead. If he looked back, for even a moment, it would slow him down, and he knew he couldn't afford to lose even a second when running for his life.

Never had Rairai guessed he could run so fast or so long as he weaved in and out of side streets in attempt to lose his pursuers. It seemed like he was running forever when he finally spotted a familiar nutrition center. He knew he was now not far from the community. If only he could make it there, he'd be safe. As he rounded the curve and the sanctuary came into sight, he began to panic. The gates were closed! Running up to those big solid doors he began to pound frantically. "Open up! It's me, Rairai! Let me in!"

It was then that Rairai turned to look behind him. He could see that about ten men were chasing him. They had now stopped running and were just casually walking towards him, their faces scarred with hungry wicked grins. A couple of them seemed to be carrying some sort of makeshift weapons in their hands.

Turning back to the gate, he continued to pound upon it. "Open up! Open up!" he shouted, all the while knowing that the men were moving ever closer. "Please, open the gates!" he pleaded desperately, when suddenly, he felt someone pulling on his arm. A familiar voice told him, "Come with me."

Rairai allowed himself to be pulled behind some underbrush at the edge of the gate, and then quickly moved along the wall. He could hear the men begin shouting again, and there was the sound of rustling as they entered the bushes behind them.

"Through here," Atira told him.

Rairai followed her through the opening in the wall. "But they are coming," he said, once inside. From the sound of their voices, he could tell they were not far off.

"Don't worry," Atira told him. She then took out her quantum-eraser and with a quick adjustment to the settings, instantly filled in the opening with a conglomeration of random protons pulled from the air. The result was a strange messy looking fix, but it was strong, and it was impenetrable. No one would be able to break through.

Realizing that he was finally safe, Rairai sighed and then collapsed on the ground. His legs felt like they were on fire. "Oh Atira," he gasped, "I...thought...the end...of me." He could hear the muffled sounds of his angry pursuers on the other side of the wall.

"You are home now," Atira reassured him as she crouched down and softly touched his forehead.

Instantly, Rairai found his breathing returning to normal and his legs no longer aching. He looked at Atira in surprise. "Did you just...? My legs...there's no pain?"

Atira just smiled at him and asked, "Why did you not return immediately? You would have had time to get away after everything broke open. I made sure of that."

"I...I just had something to do," he replied, still shaken from what he had done and not sure if he wanted to talk about it.

"Did you kill him?" she asked.

At first, Rairai was not sure if he should say it out loud. He had just killed a Noblatj and there was no crime greater in his world. It surprised him that, even after all that had happened...all that he now knew, there were still remnants of that old order in his mind holding him back. He pushed those remnants aside and said, "I almost didn't. When I was faced with him like that. In the flesh. It wasn't like it was in my fantasies. I...I think I might have let him live, but he tried to kill me first. He admitted to killing Twydi and then he tried to kill me. But he's gone. Now Bitterridge is gone for good. Maybe everything is gone for good. It's madness out there, Atira. I know you said these changes were for a better world, but can this world recover from this? You saw what it is like out there."

Atira stood up then offered him her hand. Rairai reached out and took it. She gently pulled him to his feet, surprising him with her strength.

"Don't worry," she reassured him. "Not only will your world be rebuilt, but it will be better than you could ever possibly imagine."

CHAPTER 65

"Where have you been?" asked Taqwi who was standing in the foyer. "The people have been very worried."

Atira knew the people were not really panicked. It was just Taqwi feeling a little embarrassed to admit that it had been him who had been worrying. "Everything is fine," she reassured him. "There was something that needed to be finished. It is now over and it's time to move on to the next step. Follow me. There is something we need to do together." She then quickly headed up the stairs with Taqwi close behind.

As they reached the top of the stairs, Taqwi said, "The gates are secure and everyone inside is safe, but we need to do something about what is happening outside. How will we begin to fix that?"

"Come with me," said Atira, taking him by his hand and leading him into her room. There, she guided him over to her console. "Sit," she instructed, and he sat in her chair.

Next, she ran her hand over the console and a panel popped up. "Do you see this?" she asked.

"That's the Central Bureau for the Noblatjs. It's headquarters for the entire planet."

"Yes, the Noblatj's control center"

Taqwi could see the massive dila-glass security doors had been smashed in. Not even the Central Bureau had been safe from the rioting Lessers.

Atira pulled up another panel, revealing the interior of the building. Taqwi was even more shocked by what he was seeing. This great formidable center of power, that Lessers had feared and dreaded for as long as anyone could remember, was now only a pitiful abandoned wreck. Furniture was broken and strewn everywhere, artwork destroyed, consoles smashed. The rioters had not held back. "What I want to show you should be down this way," Atira told him, as she moved the display deeper into the building.

Taqwi watched in fascination. It became obvious that no area in the Bureau had been spared. All along the way, doors had been smashed, debris was everywhere, and graffiti was scrawled on the walls.

NO MORE NOBLATJS
NOBLATJS ARE LIARS
THE END OF THE NOBLATJS

After zigging and zagging through several narrow hallways and down some stairs, Taqwi was surprised when he saw they were now looking at what was obviously the janitorial section. There were scrubbers, polishers and cupboards labelled with cleaning supplies. It seemed to be the only place in the building that was untouched by looters.

"This is it," Atira said, adjusting the image so that now they were staring at a simple door with the words, **'TOXIC WASTE: DO NOT ENTER'**, printed in bold red letters.

Pressing her hand against the panel as if she were pressing on the actual opening mechanism, the door on the screen slid open. Taqwi was amazed and wondered how she could have possibly combined the virtual image and the real world in that way.

"Now, we need to physically go there, but we need to do it through quantum travel. It's like I did before, only this time it will not just be me. We will synchronize our desire and we will travel together. Take my hand and believe with me," she instructed Taqwi. "If you need to close your eyes to concentrate, that is alright. But you must have faith so that we can move through space and time."

Taqwi wasn't sure if he fully understood what she wanted. How do you synchronize your thoughts with an alien or with anyone for that matter? And quantum travel? How do you even begin? He stared at her outstretched hand. Could he believe the way she wanted him to? Did he have that much faith in his own heart?

Placing his hand in hers, he closed his eyes and tried hard to think about moving with her to that room shown on the screen. He envisioned them together, floating, flying, coming to rest in that place. After a few seconds, nothing seemed to be happening, so he tried concentrating even harder, but then, to his surprise, found himself falling into thoughts of how beautiful her hand felt in his own. The softness and warmth of her skin, her long slender fingers… it was so joyous to be with her…so close…so intimate. He felt like he was being enveloped by something wonderful…something similar to before…something incredible. Suddenly, Atira said, "Open your eyes."

Taqwi opened them and was shocked to find he was no longer sitting in Atira's room but was now standing in front of the open door in the Central Bureau. "We did it! We actually did it!" he exclaimed with amazed laughter.

Still holding his hand, Atira said, "Remember back when you and the children were almost arrested in the shop and I managed to instantly reach you, and when you asked how I did it, I explained that it was quantum travel? Well, it was by your faith that I was able to do it the first time, and it is by the combination of your faith and mine that we, together, were able to do this now. It is a wonderful and very rare thing to have occurred. I cannot begin to tell you how special it is. It has a larger effect in the universe. It changes things for the better. Opens doors. Exalts life over death. It's all very complicated and too difficult to fully explain at this moment, so let's just go inside. There is something we need to do here." Atira then released his hand and he followed her in through the door.

As they stood at the top of the stairs and looked out over the enormous completely white room, Taqwi was astounded by what he saw. There, before him, was a seemingly endless sea of consoles with open panels showing images of streets and houses and businesses. Of course, he knew about the cameras everywhere, but to see this, the headquarters where the entire world was observed, it was suddenly so real.

"The Noblatjs called this their 'Den of Eyes'," explained Atira. She then headed down the stairs with Taqwi following after.

"If they had all this surveillance, why did they know nothing of us…of you?" he asked.

"There were times when I thwarted their spying abilities," explained Atira. "But also greed and arrogance blinded them. In wanting more and more power, they overextended themselves. With so many observation screens, they could no longer focus on anything. There was simply too much information to make sense of any of it. Also, they felt so above everyone else on this planet that our community was able to grow right under their noses. We were only Lessers, capable of very little in their minds. If they noticed us at all, the only thing they would have seen would have been ordinary people doing ordinary things. In their arrogance, whenever they saw me, all they could see was a simple woman attracted to wealthy Lessers. They couldn't even begin to imagine how much more we are."

Taqwi laughed and said, "We are the invisible force."

"Yes, we are," Atira replied. "Now watch what this force can do." She then took out the quantum-eraser and waved it once over the room. Instantly, all the screens, the consoles and even the chairs disappeared. They now stood in a large empty white hall. Taqwi was silent with disbelief. It's gone! It's really all gone!

"There is one more thing we must do here," said Atira her voice now echoing throughout the empty chamber. "Something very important. Come this way."

Taqwi followed her to the very end of the great room where a plain unassuming door hung on archaic hinges. She pushed down on the antique handle and opened it. "This is where it all begins," she told him.

This room was entirely white like the other, but much smaller. It housed only a single, but very large console, along with a very comfortable looking high-backed chair. "Sit down," said Atira.

Taqwi walked over and sat down in the chair. Atria then opened a panel and he stared at the large blank screen in front of him. "What do I do now?" he asked a little nervously.

"This place is called the Image Center," said Atira. "It is hooked up to every electronic device on this planet. From here, you can broadcast to screens and infolios everywhere. You, Taqwi, are their new leader who will put things back together the good way...the balanced way."

It took Taqwi a minute to realize what she was telling him. The new leader? "But wait!" he protested. "Yes, I thought about what you said earlier about me leading the planet, but I don't think I can do it. I mean, who am I? There must be someone better? The whole world? Me the leader?" Taqwi was suddenly terrified at the idea and the great responsibility.

Atira sighed and gently brushed a strand of hair from his forehead. "This is exactly why you are the leader. Do you think this world needs another arrogant fool who would simply set up the same system over again? They need someone like you. Kind. Caring. Empathetic. Someone who knows what this planet needs and isn't about to let his ego get in the way. Someone who can stand strong as a natural sentinel against Moloch returning. No one else will do, Taqwi. You are the best candidate on this planet."

Taqwi sat for a moment in silence, not knowing what to say. Could he really lead the entire planet? And a planet in such chaos?

"Now," said Atira. "It is time to introduce yourself to the world. You will tell them about the changes ahead. You will reassure them. You will speak of community and working together. You will explain that no longer are there any Noblatjs or Lessers. There are now only people...one people living together on a fair and thriving world. You can do this, Taqwi. Like I said before, all that you need is within you and all you have to do is release it."

Taqwi took in a deep breath. For years, he had dreamt of living in a world such as the one Atira was describing. Was it really now happening? Do dreams really come true? He thought about the chaos going on outside and about the community he had built. Definitely, something had to be done, and Atira, who had been right about everything else, seemed to think that he was the only one who could do it. He couldn't just walk away because he was a frightened by the responsibility. No, he had to summon up the courage to at least try. For the community, for the children, for the future of his planet, he had to at least try.

"When I switch the connector on, you will see your own image reflected there. That is what will appear on every screen everywhere."

"But what do I say?" Taqwi asked, worried about making such an important impromptu speech.

"Speak from your heart because your heart is a very good place. Good words will flow from there," she told him then leaned in and kissed his cheek.

Taqwi sighed as he remembered their mind-merge. It was not simply about the pleasure of it. This merging had left him different. It had infused within him a new energy...a new focus. Atira was right. What he needed was inside of him. There was no need to be afraid or to doubt himself. Sitting up straight and facing the screen, he thought about what he would say. *From the heart.* That's all he had to remember. Speak from the heart and the words will come. He took in a deep breath said, "I'm ready."

Atira pressed an icon on the console and Taqwi suddenly came face to face with himself. His gentle eyes looked startled for a moment as they stared back at him, but he quickly regained his composure and said, "Hello. My name is Taqwi and I am here to let you know that you should not feel anxious or afraid. Something wonderful is happening to our planet! Something that we have waited on for a very long time. It's good news for everyone! So, put away all your anger and your frustration. Now is a time of celebration...of rejoicing, for a new and beautiful world is being born...a world of fairness and justice where there are no Lessers or Noblatjs. There are only people...a thriving progressive people...the kind who turn their backs on no one...the kind whose hearts and minds are always open...the kind who believe in each other and are open to new and better ways. This is the kind of people we are and the kind of world that is now possible..."

CHAPTER 66

Atira watched as the children laughed and ran about in the garden. The community gates remained locked for now as the chaos outside was still dying down, but she knew that soon they would be opened. For the moment, these children who had suffered so much hardship and pain could play happily within their little sanctuary, but it wouldn't be long before their new world would be ready. The gates would be flung open, and they would be able to experience all the wonder of a planet full of hope and progress.

She leaned her head against the old tree that had grown there long before she had ever built this house. It, in fact, had been the sign that had first drawn her to this spot as the place to build. It was far older than the neighborhood, and even than the entire city. Rooted in that rich earth long before the planet had been divided into Noblatjs and Lessers, it contained the purity of the original... the world's virgin origins.

Atira remembered back to the moment when she had despaired and lost faith in the possibility that the planet could be saved. Yes, this world with its cold harsh ways had thrown her into the pit of despair, but she had climbed out again, and now another mission had been successfully completed. She looked up at the bright beautiful sky, smiled and thought of her Naomh. She knew he was well pleased.

"It's a lovely day," Rairai said as he walked up from behind and stood beside her.

Atira turned her head and looked at his face. Although mostly healed, there remained a small mark on his cheek from the scratches he received when running from the mob. "It's a very lovely day," she replied.

Rairai watched the children happily playing. "You're definitely the boss, so tell me, what's next? Where do I go from here?"

Atira surprised him when she gently took his hand and said, "For you, it's time to change. Lofty Bitterridge is dead. The old world is gone. You cannot go back to who you were before. Change your name, how you look, everything. Taqwi will need the help of good people. You are a good man, Rairai, perhaps you can help him."

"Are you sure?" he asked her. "The wealthy Lesser who swindled the entire world? Am I truly redeemable? Am I good enough?"

"That you would even ask that question tells me you are," she replied. "You feel ashamed for what you have done, and you've repented. You've learned and evolved."

"I hope so," Rairai said. "I really want to be good enough." He then wondered about Atira's plans for herself. "And will you remain here on this planet? Will you stay and help us rebuild?" he asked.

"A ship will come for me in a few days. What I came here to do, has been finished. I have added balance to the universe and shone a light in the darkness. An evil force has been defeated in this place, and it is time for me to return to my own planet. If I stayed here, away from my home, I would eventually die. I must leave so that I may live on."

Rairai then did something that surprised even him. He grabbed her in his arms and kissed her. As soon as he had realized what he had done, he stepped back in embarrassment. "I'm sorry," he said. "I don't know why I did that. It's just that, I have never met anyone like you. The things you have done. The hope that you've given us here. Releasing us from the oppression of the Noblatjs. Just look at how happy the children are. I...I was carried away by the moment, I suppose. I'm sorry."

Atira was very surprised by his sudden burst of passion. It was something similar to what she had felt from Zylong but was also very different. This passion was genuine and came from the heart. It didn't want to take from her. It only wanted to give something. It was the difference between sweet longing and greed.

"In a different time and place," she told him, "we could have been together, but I must return home, and you have a planet to help rebuild. From time to time, I will need to look in on this world, to ensure that Moloch is not nesting here again. When I do, I will always be sure to look in on you, Rairai Swyer."

"But I will have a different name," he smiled. "How will you find me?"

"I will always find you," she laughed. "Just like when, as a boy, you found me in your daydreams."

Rairai was confused by what she had just said. "Daydreams? What do you mean? What daydreams are you talking about? How could I find you in my daydreams?"

"Multi-dimensional mind travel," she explained. "Do you remember the wolar?"

"My imaginary wolar?" laughed Rairai. "I used to drive my parents crazy with that imaginary creature."

"Not so imaginary," Atira said.

"What do you mean, the wolar was not imaginary?"

"Did you ever wonder why you had so much faith in me…a stranger? Have you ever trusted anyone as much as you trusted me? You did not even trust Twydi to that extent. Because travel to other planets can block out memories, I did not recognize you in the beginning, but now I remember. You don't remember me, but I remember you. The time we wrestled on the beach and I scratched your leg. It made you cry, and I felt badly for what I had done. Do you remember that?"

Rairai shook his head in disbelief. "No, how could this be? Of course, I remember. You are saying that you were my…my wolar?"

Atira smiled at him, "There is motion and there is rest. In playing with a little boy on the beach, I found rest. We connected in a different dimension so that we might meet one day in this one."

"So, you set it all up?" he asked.

"Not exactly. It was a part of my Naomh's plans."

"What's a Naomh?"

"My Naomh is…how shall I explain…my Naomh is inside of me and outside of me…the center of the universe…the universe itself. I am because of my Naomh. All the good parts of you and this planet are also because of my Naomh."

"I don't understand," said Rairai.

"You don't have to," Atira told him. "You don't have to understand any of it. Just know that your world is not only safe from destruction, but it is a better place for everyone here. Your job now is to keep it that way. Are you prepared to commit yourself to this?"

"Yes," he replied. It was true that the old Rairai had been selfish and deceitful, but now it was time for him to take responsibility and become a more giving and caring person. "I will not let my planet down and I will not let you down," he said. "I promise you that."

CHAPTER 67

Taqwi leaned back in his chair and closed his eyes. It was the first time in a long time that he had found a moment to himself. There was so much to be done...so much to organize. Not that he wasn't enjoying it...watching the new world take shape...seeing the people they once called Lessers rising up and displaying their long-suppressed talents. The planet was coming together and quickly evolving into a much more egalitarian society. Everyone now had homes and food, and there was a new sense of responsibility for one another.

At first, he had worried that the transition would be difficult for people. They had lived such a long time in an oppressive world. How would they adjust? But he found their adaptation was progressing quite smoothly. The Noblatjs had created an unnatural unbalanced order and now the planet was naturally returning to what it was intended to be. All the pieces were falling freely into place. The people were finding their way instinctively.

"Are you tired?" a voice said from behind him.

Taqwi smiled, "We all need to take a little time to rest," he said, spinning around and rising out of his chair. He now stood face to face with Atira.

"I'm going home soon," she told him.

"When?" he asked, hoping she wouldn't notice how sad this news made him feel.

"A ship should arrive in a few days."

"I'd love to come on board, just to see what your ship is like."

"I'm sorry, Taqwi, but you can't. The atmosphere inside is from my world. It is not meant to sustain someone from yours. I can only breathe on your planet because of an implant."

Taqwi laughed, "You really are an alien, aren't you?"

Atira took his hand gently in her own. "Actually, you and everyone on this planet are the aliens."

Taqwi laughed even harder. "I want to thank you for what you have done here."

"*Thank you!*" she exclaimed. "On the day you first arrived at my door, I did not realize how you would be the one this planet needed. You proved yourself over and over again. Without you, I don't know if I would have been able to defeat Moloch or at least defeat the beast this quickly." Atira then surprised them both by giving him a very long and passionate kiss. His lips tasted of hope and renewal. Something she had longed to taste since her arrival on the planet. It tasted wonderful!

Taqwi wrapped his arms tightly around her and held her close. "I love you," he whispered into her ear, "I know that you have to go, but before you do, I just wanted you to know that I love you."

Suddenly, Atira felt a wellspring of emotion rise up within her. For a moment, she didn't know what was happening, but then she realized. This was it! It all finally made sense. Zylong…her pain… the searching…the struggle. This was the secret door within herself that needed to be opened. It was so secret even she knew nothing about it. Now, because of Taqwi's true declaration of pure honest love, it had been flung open, and with that, a new energy was suddenly flowing out of her and enveloping the entire planet. She could feel it! It was glorious!

Taqwi felt it too. He stepped back and looked at her in wonderment. "What's happening, Atira? It's as if the ground is shaking…but it's the sky too! Everything is shaking! And it's so bright! Everything is so bright! And it feels…Atira, it feels incredible! What is this about?"

"Isn't it wonderful!" Atira exclaimed, taking his hands in her own. "It's freedom! The mystery has finally been revealed and now I know that this planet will not only be free of Moloch, but it will become a shining beacon in the universe. And all it took, Taqwi, was for you to love me. Honestly and purely. Now all that love I held inside of myself for so long has been freed and is washing this world clean! You did it Taqwi! For me, for this world and for yourself! You have broken the seal and released the glorious light! I love you Taqwi! I love this world! I love! I love! I love!"

www.ingramcontent.com/pod-product-compliance
Lightning Source LLC
Chambersburg PA
CBHW070017120726
47909CB00003B/973